LOST DAWNS

PREQUEL NOVELLA TO THE LOST MILLENNIUM TRILOGY

MIKE SHEPHERD

KL & MM BOOKS

Lost Dawns: Prequel Novella to the Lost Millennium Trilogy

Published by KL & MM Books
July, 2017

This book is a work of fiction set 2000 years in humanity's past. Any similarity between present people, places or events would be spectacularly unlikely and is purely coincidental.

This book is written and published by the author. Please don't pirate it. I'm self-employed. The money I earn from the sales of these books allows me to produce more stories to entertain you. I'd hate to have to get a day job again. If this book comes into your hands free, please consider going to your favorite e-book provider and investing in a copy so I can continue to earn a living at this wonderful art.

I would like to thank my wonderful cover artist, Scott Grimando, who did all my Ace covers and will continue doing my own book covers. I also am grateful for the editing skill of Lisa Müller, David Vernon Houston, Edee Lemonier, and, as ever, Ellen Moscoe.

V 1.0

eBook ISBN-13: 978-164211-0197
Print ISBN-13: 978-164211-0258

ALSO BY MIKE SHEPHERD

Published by KL & MM Books

Kris Longknife: Admiral

Kris Longknife: Emissary

Kris Longknife's Successor

Kris Longknife's Replacement

Kris Longknife's Relief

Rita Longknife: Enemy Unknown

Rita Longknife: Enemy in Sight

Short Stories from KL & MM Books

Kris Longknife's Maid Goes On Strike and Other Short Stories:
Vignettes from Kris Longknife's World

Kris Longknife's Maid Goes On Strike

Kris Longknife's Bad Day

Ruth Longknife's First Christmas

Kris Longknife: Among the Kicking Birds

Ace Books by Mike Shepherd

Kris Longknife: Mutineer

Kris Longknife: Deserter

Kris Longknife: Defiant

Kris Longknife: Resolute

Kris Longknife: Audacious

Kris Longknife: Intrepid

Kris Longknife: Undaunted

Kris Longknife: Redoubtable

Kris Longknife: Daring

Kris Longknife: Furious

Kris Longknife: Defender

Kris Longknife: Tenacious

Kris Longknife: Unrelenting

Kris Longknife: Bold

Vicky Peterwald: Target

Vicky Peterwald: Survivor

Vicky Peterwald: Rebel

Mike Shepherd writing as Mike Moscoe in the Jump Point Universe

First Casualty

The Price of Peace

They Also Serve

Rita Longknife: To Do or Die

Short Specials

Kris Longknife: Training Daze

Kris Longknife : Welcome Home, Go Away

Kris Longknife's Bloodhound

Kris Longknife's Assassin

The Lost Millennium Trilogy Published by KL & MM Books

PROLOGUE

One year ago.

The young scientist stood up, and turned his back on the microscope and its evidence.

"It did not work."

He stepped aside. The older man came, took off his glasses, stared at the screen of the electron microscope. He fiddled with its dials, as if changing the focus might somehow change the results.

"It did not work," the senior scientist finally echoed. His words held a finality that replaced the tentativeness of the junior.

"Maybe it is just as well." The young man shrugged.

"The Leader wants it." The old one's eyes went hard with duty and determination.

"Yes." The subordinate did not add the 'but,' though it hung in the air between them. The older man's fingers circled the mottling that disfigured his face, marking him for death. "The Leader wants this and the Leader will have it." His gaze wandered the room, settling on the ceiling fan as it toiled to stir the hot, humid air of the laboratory.

His voice became distant. "I have buried my wife. I have buried my sons and my daughters and their children. It is time for those people to stand beside a grave."

The young man turned away from him, his stomach in knots. If the Leader had his way there might be too few left alive to dig the graves. He looked again at the microscope.

Maybe the Leader's will could not be done.

The older man's eyes came into focus. "I have an idea."

1

Yesterday

Bakuza Qwabes shivered as the perspiration ran down his back. The heat and humidity of the day did not reach into the marble and granite inner sanctum. Cold seeped up through the soles of his shoes from the very stones he walked on. But the temperature had nothing to do with the shivers Bakuza struggled to suppress.

Across the vast expanse of unfeeling stone was the Leader. Once this had been the largest church in Christendom. Now it was the seat of power for most of Africa. For Bakuza, whose only faith was in the will of the people and service to the Leader, the building was being put to better use – or so he had said many times.

Only now he approached the leader for the first time. Now he walked the cold marble. Enormous slabs of granite rose on either side, drawing his eyes upward, shrinking him to nothingness. He could hear men working in the offices that had been built into the side naves, but his eyes were drawn straight ahead. Where the sanctuary had once been, where the altar had stood, now loomed a massive stone table that the Leader used as a desk. Behind it sat a huge ebony chair, its back decorated with carvings of Africans being brutalized by Europeans.

"You have good news for me." The Leader did not turn to face Bakuza, yet his strong baritone filled the huge room, reverberating off the stone walls, shaking Bakuza's soul.

"Our laboratories have created the weapon you called for."

"You have done well. The Europeans did nothing while AIDS ravaged our people. Now let them suffer from it. Let them bury *their* dead."

The fast acting, airborne plague that the laboratory now grew was not exactly the AIDS virus the Leader had demanded. Bakuza did not correct the Leader, just as he did not pass along the fear of the younger biologist that this plague might not leave enough alive to bury the dead. Bakuza had never before stood in the presence of the Leader, but he knew not to contradict him.

The chair swivelled around. Bakuza Qwabes saw the Leader's face for the first time.

His master's satisfied grin was that of a hungry lion that sees its next kill. "You have done very well, my son. We will find a place for you on my personal staff."

C adet Launa O'Brian double-timed up the familiar gray steps of Washington Hall. Behind her, spring was launching its first belated offensive, breaking out into a riot of smells and colors with plants too weak to camouflage a tank or track. Behind her, as she passed the second floor, half the classrooms were empty, silent proof West Point's class of 1999 would be half the size of the class that saw the last decade in.

But it was not Launa's way to look behind her. She was one of four in the running for First Captain. She would not be the first woman to command the Brigade, but it would be one thing the Colonel had never done. The look on her father's face when she first led the Brigade in review would be something to remember for a lifetime.

She halted before the Commandant's office. Positive no infraction had caused the summons from her afternoon class, still, she prepared herself for any eventuality. Quickly, she ran one hand over her hair. She had spent much of her high school years searching for a hairstyle that was efficient but feminine; the jog across campus should not have put one honey blond lock out of place.

Firmly she pulled down her uniform tunic, its tight lines were not broken by unmilitary excess baggage. She prided herself on the small breasts of a gymnast. She had been building upper body strength since the day she turned thirteen and decided to be a soldier. That month, a woman had shown she could command men in combat down Panama way. Kuwait had given her more role models. Three years back, Congress had finally revised the law. After graduation, it was "Airborne All the Way" for Launa and command of a rifle platoon.

She modified the angle of her hat brim. Confident she looked the part of a Commander of the Brigade, she squared her corners as she marched to the door, opened it, and entered the Commandant's outer office.

Before she could report her presence, Mrs. Hammon, the civilian secretary, recognized her and keyed the intercom. "She's here." Launa got a worried, hurried, and distracted look and a quick, "Please go in."

That was not what Launa expected. Facing the oak door that sealed the inner sanctum, she had a moment of apprehension, but she knocked three times and entered by the numbers. Closing the door behind her, she smartly stepped off the two paces to the front of the Commandant's desk. If someone took a protractor to the angles of her hand salute, they might find that she was off by a quarter of a degree here or there. Then again, they might not.

Launa would take the bet.

"Cadet O'Brian reporting as ordered, Sir." She held her salute until Major General William G. Patterson, USA, returned it, then assumed the exaggerated brace she had become used to over the last three years.

"At ease, cadet."

She switched to that tight military posture that was anything but. Without moving a facial muscle, she let her eyes take in the third person in the room.

A man lounged against the wall to the left of the General's desk. He looked to be about five eight, three inches taller than her and maybe eight years her senior. His frame did not show an ounce of excess fat or muscle. The uniform of an U.S. Army captain showed jumper's wings, Combat Infantry Badge and a Ranger patch. Somebody thought he was good. Growing up Army, she had met enough careerists whose "merit badges' only showed they were good at getting their ticket punched. She would reserve judgment. The name badge said BEAR.

"Cadet." The General got her undivided attention. "You are the leader of a Neolithic town of 2,000 souls. One thousand are adult females and males, farmers, herders and crafts workers, experienced in physical labor and capable of providing military service." Launa noted the General neutered each noun.

"Your people have no military training or background. Your enemy is light cavalry, born to the saddle, the bow and to conquest. How would you defend?" The General fixed her with a gaze that could melt obsidian.

Launa blinked, and froze her face before a frown could betray her puzzlement.

What kind of silly drill was this? Something like this had come up last week in an Anthropology Lecture. Major Henderson had outlined the challenges to the Old Europeans of 4,000 B.C. with the same brevity that she used in her Battle and Tactics lectures.

Launa had flashed anger at a feminine led society that failed so miserably to meet a new challenge. She had recognized the futility of her anger when a classmate whispered, "Chill out, Launa. What's the use of being pissed at folks that have been dust for 6,000 years?"

She had laughed with him, and regained her perspective.

In the time it took her to swallow and moisten a pair of suddenly dry vocal cords, she began outlining the tactical solution she had devised that night over a coke with her friend after anthropology class.

"Archeological finds show that the opposition was lightly equipped cavalry. They used short bows as missile weapons. When they closed for shock combat, they used javelins and dagger-length bronze short swords. Since they lacked the stirrup, shock weapons would only be used at the dismount. For all practical purposes, that's also the best way to use the bow. What we have here are dragoons, with the horse providing strategic mobility and tactical engagement taking place on foot."

Out of the corner of her eye, Launa caught the Captain covering his mouth with his hand, but his cheeks betrayed the smirk he was trying to cover. Just who was this guy? As her cadet buddy said, these folks were 6,000 years dead. The General might as well have been a bronze statue for all the reaction he showed.

"I'd arm the light infantry with slings. Slingers have several advantages. Many herders would have used it to protect their sheep from predators. This weapon is deadly in the hands of either a man or woman. David reputedly brought down an experienced warrior at an age when his upper body strength would not have been more than the average woman's. Slings have a range advantage over a short bow, possibly quite significant, depending on the weight of the stone. Lastly, it's all non-strategic material."

Launa found her excitement rising. She enjoyed sinking her teeth into this kind of problem.

"My shock troops would use pikes ten to sixteen feet long. I'd employ a mixed tactical formation of men and women. The enemy is light cavalry; their body armor is probably limited to boiled leather. It's unlikely the horses have any. Such a force cannot carry home a charge against a wall of pikes. Once the horsemen are afoot, the pikes can deal with their short swords at a reasonable distance. The Old Europeans would not have to pay the heavy civic price the macho hoplite demanded for facing his enemy at short spear point."

Launa hoped her use of "macho" would not get her in trouble. However, the heavy psychological price of shock combat on a community had to be considered. Men who'd faced off with other men at sword point expected a lot when they got home, and women were always the ones at home giving.

According to Major Henderson, the women and men of the mid-Neolithic lived as peers. Launa needed a combat system that would let them fight and, if necessary, die the way the Major said they lived.

Personally, Launa questioned the historical validity of the Major's lecture. Peaceful kingdoms were for fairy tales. She had taken it as a challenging tactical problem. Based on her knowledge of six thousand years of man's inhumanity, she had formulated a solid solution to the problem.

Launa's enthusiasm for this exercise was having its impact. She realized her stance, while never exactly breaking the minimum requirements of "At Ease," had relaxed. Her head bobbed a bit, in cadence with her words.

The General sported the merest hint of a smile at the corners of his mouth.

The Captain watched her intently, the lines around his eyes becoming more pronounced; he no longer lounged against the wall.

Launa launched into the final element of her tactical system.

"I'd put the engineers of my city state to work ditching the perimeter of the town. The dirt would form a wall. This fortification would serve several purposes. The slingers would have a height advantage over the bowmen, giving them extra range. The wall would channelize the assault. I'd form the pikes to protect the entrances with their flanks on the walls. With pickets stationed to give early warning, no light cavalry mustered could take my fortress."

Launa let a tight, proud grin cross her face. She was as willing to defend the elegance of her solution as she was to defend the town.

For a moment, the General rocked slowly in his chair. Then a smile broke across his face. He nodded to the Captain. "That says it all. It's within one percent of my own deployment. You got any questions for her?"

The Captain's mouth was a stern frown. "You assume the opposition is armed with a short bow. Why?"

If he wanted to shoot questions at her, she could shoot answers right back. Digging in for a rapid-fire exchange, Launa resumed a taut stance, but turned her head to face him. "First, short bows are the standard cavalry weapon. Mounted troopers would find a long bow unwieldy. Second, archaeologists simply report bows found in chieftain tombs, not long bows."

He paused only a moment to weigh her response. "Archaeologists are not soldiers. Do you trust their assessment of any weapon they find?"

"No, Sir. I do not." Launa quickly conceded the point.

The Captain gave her a shallow nod, and resumed the questioning. "Why not equip your citizen soldiers with bows?"

"To be effective with a bow requires long hours of practice. This usually means a professional warrior class. I want to avoid that. Also, I'd expect to find experience with the sling in the labor pool."

"Wouldn't the range of a long bow be worth the social price?

"Not in my opinion. Also, a composite bow requires technology I would not expect to find then and which I do not personally have." Launa hoped that would settle the matter. This guy really liked bows and arrows.

"How many miles can you run?"

"I do four miles in thirty minutes every day, Sir."

"How many chin-ups?"

"A set of 30," Launa paused for a second, "wearing a twenty-five-pound weight."

The Captain turned to the General. "I have no objections, Sir."

The General's face got somber as he took a deep breath and let it out slowly. He leaned forward in his chair, his hands folded on the desk in front of him. "Sit down, Launa. You too, Jack."

As the Colonel's daughter, Launa had relaxed around generals, their wives and family, with a natural familiarity that bred comfort. For the last three years, when Cadet O'Brian sat in a general's presence, it was at a brace. Knowing her place gave the position a psychological comfort it lacked physically. Now, suddenly, she was unsure. Generals did not address cadets by their first name.

As she fumbled with her thoughts and her chair, she watched the Captain out of the corner of her eye. He folded himself into his seat and sat with the poise of a lion, comfortable, alert, at rest – yet ready to explode into action. She tried to imitate him.

"Launa, I knew your father. He served under me two, no three, times. I knew your dad too, Jack. You couldn't ask for a better boonie rat up-country in Nam. Too bad about him." The General paused for a moment and studied them both. Launa had the uncanny feeling he was trying to memorize them. Finally, he reached for a large manila envelope on his desk. He pulled out a thick sheaf of papers. Glancing at them, he grimaced and laid them down in front of him.

"Launa, I have your orders for active duty. It doesn't say where or why. This little yellow note, hand-written by the Chief of Staff himself, says I don't have to give them to you unless you volunteer. I've been involved in some peculiar goings on in my thirty-eight years with this man's . . . this person's Army." He scowled as he corrected himself.

"Jack Walking Bear tells me that you are being detached to a unit that is involved in a contingency plan. It may never be used. If it is activated, it will be at the personal command of the President. If these orders are ever executed, and the Captain refuses to tell me anything about what those orders may be. . ." The glare the General gave Bear should have incinerated him where he sat. The Captain remained impervious. "*If* these orders are ever executed, you will be considered as dead to all who ever knew you."

Launa permitted herself a puzzled frown at the strange phrasing. The General shook his head. "Damned if I know what they're talking about." He paused for a moment, obviously uncomfortable in his ignorance. "Launa, why don't you take the afternoon to think this over? Go ask the tombstones over in the post cemetery what they think."

Launa nodded, a part of her thinking this was a

good time for a walk under the trees, a good time to reread the words on some tombstones and think. Unfortunately, another part of Launa had dreamed of a moment like this. Before she knew it, her mouth was open.

"I'm ready now, Sir. When do we leave?"

For a second the General sat frozen. Then a satisfied grin swept across his face. Launa tried to memorize it. She would never see her father's face as she took command of the Brigade. This would be the look of approval she would carry for a lifetime.

The Captain reminded her that it might be a short memory. He exploded from his chair for the doorway. "Mrs. Hammon, call the heliport. Have the chopper start rotating. Also, have our bird at Newburgh get cleared for immediate take off."

He turned back to Launa. "Let's go, Lieutenant."

Stunned by her decision, the rank, and the Captain's speed, Launa slowly got to her feet. The General reached across the desk, extending his hand. She shook it. Then he stood and saluted her. She had started to turn, obedient to the Captain's summons.

She found herself fumbling to return the salute.

The General chuckled and tossed her orders to her. "Catch! You'll need these."

Launa caught them and broke into a run. The Captain was already half way down the hall. The pace he set was a flat-out dash, but this was her territory. She knew how fast the high gloss polish on the floor would let her run.

Launa caught up with him on the stairwell and broke into daylight at his elbow. A Blackhawk sat on the Plain's helipad, blades picking up speed. They went through the doorway together. The crew chief slammed it shut behind them a second later. Launa was buckling in as the chopper lifted off.

She craned her neck, and, with a sigh, watched The Point disappear. For three years it had been her home, the longest she had ever lived in one place.

Remembering the orders in her lap, she pulled out one copy and skimmed it. The Captain was right. She was now a Second Lieutenant in the United States Army Reserve.

The orders went vague beyond that.

She looked up at the Captain, seated across from her. Leaning toward him, she shouted above the engine roar.

"Now can you tell me what this is all about?"

3

C aptain John Samuel Walking Bear studied the young woman across from him. He had set a fast pace on the way out. The last report said the weather was closing in and he did not want to waste a night grounded on the East coast. She had proven she had the smarts in the Commandant's office, now she had shown she had the muscles.

When she leaned toward him, he bent forward to hear her over the chopper's noise. "Let's wait until we can talk before we tackle that. Okay, Lieutenant?"

She frowned at his delay, but the reference to her rank drew a grin. "When do I get a pair of gold bars and a uniform to put them on?"

"We'll have a full kit waiting for you."

She nodded and sat back, watching the terrain pass below.

Walking Bear watched her and liked what he saw. He had read her medical reports and background. She had been his second choice until Captain Mendoza showed up

Monday sporting a diamond ring. Project specifications called for no local attachments.

Mendoza was dropped before she even knew the Pentagon computer had spit out her name.

So, chance would choose his partner. Chance had dealt him some bad hands in the past. God knows, he was due for a good break. From what he had seen so far of the Lieutenant, she was not a bad second choice. She rode the air turbulence with a relaxed ease. He admitted with a wry grin that she was also a pleasant eyeful.

Life could deal a man worse.

They transferred from helicopter to C-12 Gulfstream jet at a run, just as the rain began to pour. The plane rolled before the door was secured and banked steeply to avoid thunderheads on the climb out.

They had the cabin to themselves. As they buckled into seats across from each other, Launa placed her orders on the table between them. Her eyes looked about to explode with questions, but her words were few. "Now can you tell me what this is all about?"

"Will you answer me one more question?" Jack pointed at the envelope in front of her. "Why'd you accept those orders?"

She frowned and paused a moment before she spoke. "A soldier can be a pretty sad creature. We don't make anything. We don't get rich. Most people don't like us. But we count when it matters. An old Roman said it for me: `The soldier stands between the torches of the enemy and the hearthstones of the people.'"

Jack admired the fire that gleamed in her eyes, but he could not help wondering what price they might pay for her idealism.

She gave an embarrassed shrug. "I know that sounds poetic, but it's the way I feel. Oh, I've met generals who weren't worth the price their gold braid would bring in a pawn shop. But we follow the sword because there are some things more important than a person's pleasure or profit. There are some ideas worth putting your life on the line for."

The words came slowly, now. She seemed to pick and polish each individually.

"You say the President wants me to put my life on the line. A soldier can go twenty years and never do anything the President gives a damn about. If I'd said no, I wouldn't be the person I want to be."

He weighed her answer for only a moment before saying, "What can I tell you?"

"Who, what, when, where, how." She waved both arms, the words poured as from a dam's open sluice gate. "Or anything else for starters."

"I'll give you a quick overview. There'll be fuller briefings tomorrow. I'll try to give you a general appreciation of what you've dealt yourself into. First, what do you know of `The Movement?'"

"Another question," she half growled, half laughed.

"Sorry. I thought the guy who did my initial briefing did a lousy job too. Now I'm feeling a lot more sympathy for him. Bear with me, okay?"

"Last week, I got Africa as an assignment." She eyed Jack. He looked innocent; he was. Someone else had done her prep work.

"My research didn't tell me much. The Movement surfaced in Africa three years back, apparently as an outgrowth of the tens of millions of deaths from AIDS which shattered the social fabric of that poor continent. The

Swahili word the media translates simply as `movement' really means 'the lion stalks'."

Jack noted the way she carefully nuanced her words. Her file said she was good at languages; they would need that. Her folks had been posted oversees several times and she had dealt with many different cultures at an early age. They shared that in common -- good.

"Unlike many earlier terrorist groups," she went on, "the Movement doesn't want to broadcast its manifesto on Western TV. They're as likely to stake a news team out on a termite hill as they are to send them back alive. Either way, they don't give interviews."

She frowned at the ceiling of the plane.

He nodded encouragement for her to go on.

"I don't know what the Movement is. I wouldn't give any of the stuff I read in the papers an intelligence confidence level above C-3."

"Lieutenant, I'll let you in on a little secret. I have read the DIA and CIA's files. There's nothing in them above C-1."

Her mouth dropped open.

Jack had had a hard time believing that one himself. There was a lot about the world situation he had trouble believing. For starters, where were the smart people who were supposed to be running it?

"The Movement is so tight the agency doesn't have a single first or even a good second-hand source. Five years ago, no one had even heard of the Movement. Today, they dominate half the governments in Africa. As for the other half..."

He tossed the unasked question off with a fatalistic shrug. He knew he was imitating his grandfather and hated it. A reservation Indian had to shrug off a lot. An infantry Captain shouldn't.

"Officially, Egypt, Libya, and the Union of South Africa are independent. The last reporter to ask who really ran Libya died in a fiery car crash." He shook his head grimly. "The CIA has no good answers either."

"Why control a country under the table?" Launa stroked her chin.

"Egypt and Libya are still buying Western arms, the latest fighters, tanks, and electronics. We've black-listed most of the countries the Movement rules openly. Ever get the feeling there's a hole in the West's arms embargo?"

Launa sat back in her seat, disgust dripping from her smile. "There are times when I wonder why soldiers even try?" After a moment's reflection, she sat forward. "If the Europeans had to defend themselves against the arms somebody is shipping south, what would they have?"

Jack approved of where her thinking was headed. "Since the Soviet government collapsed and everybody cashed in their peace dividend, the classified Order of Battle is the same as the public OB. What with Desert Storm, the budget cutters figured nobody'd be dumb enough to mess with us." They exchanged sardonic smiles at logic that eluded them. "Today, Europe and the US couldn't muster a dozen divisions."

"What does Africa have?"

"God only knows."

"And She ain't talking." Launa ventured a half smile at the old joke.

Jack broke into a broad grin.

"The joke wasn't that funny?"

"God's a woman where and when we're going."

Launa gave him a puzzled frown.

"People thought God was a woman 6,000 years ago." He expanded upon his comment.

"So?"

He had her undivided attention. "Six thousand years ago, a gentle civilization lost a war. We're going to change that." He had the past three weeks to get used to the idea. He did not have long to wait for her reaction.

"Six thousand years ago! Get real, Captain." She snorted. "Don't you think it's a little late to enlist for that campaign? I mean, last time I checked, time machines were not standard issue at the post motor pool."

Jack grinned. "I like it. You address the craziest idea in good old Army lingo. Keep your sense of humor. You'll need it. Actually, they are issuing us a time machine."

Jack watched Launa's eyes get wide as dismay swamped her face. "I'm just a combat engineer, no scientist, so I don't know a lot about the technical side. As I understand it, the machine started out as a mistake."

"A mistake?" She echoed.

"Yeah." Jack rushed to fill the silence while Launa's disbelief deepened into shock. "The Livermore Lab was doing some high energy physics stuff for Star Wars. One particular test required gigawatts, more energy than they had any right to expect to use operationally and they were on the verge of closing it down.

"But, after the last experiment, Harrison noticed the instruments were tracking emissions *before* the test run. They'd seen it before and dismissed it as storage leakage. For the last three runs, she tweaked the equipment to maximize that effect. She got her boss's curiosity up and they managed to run more tests. When they finished, they were sending several watts back as far as ten minutes before they started."

"But most of SDI closed down in the mid-90s." Launa

frowned, grasping for a handle – any handle – on this discussion.

"Right, but the world being in the energy mess it's in, energy research got extra funding. With the declassification of high energy research worldwide, we got to peek over everyone else's shoulders. Of course, our Livermore group was too busy to publish," he finished with a sly grin.

Launa shook her head slowly. "Okay, maybe you've got the equipment, but time travel is crazy."

Jack approved the speed with which she went from shock to analysis and back to the attack. He tried a new slant, "You read much science fiction?"

"Some." She sat back in her chair, furrowed eyebrows concealing what thoughts lay behind her eyes.

"A friend of mine had quite a collection when I was a kid." Jack went at this one slowly. "I'd sneak off and read it when I could. Writers from H.G. Wells on, used to toy with the problems of changing history. You know, shooting your grandpa, that sort of thing."

Launa nodded.

"Sometime in the 70s, the more informed ones discovered quantum mechanics. From then on, most said you couldn't change history – you just created a new time line."

"Yeah, that's most of what I've read. Has your Livermore friend figured out which one is right?"

"She doesn't have the foggiest idea." Jack threw his hands up.

Launa shifted in her seat and began methodically putting all the pieces together. They didn't fit. "If we are assuming, for discussion purposes only, that this mistake can be tricked together into an operational time machine, why go back to 4,000 B.C.? Assuming the Movement's worth the risk, why not send an assassin back a few ago and solve the problem before it starts?"

Her distaste for this solution dripped from each word, but her idealism did not stop her from voicing the logic of expedience.

Good.

Jack had expected this line of attack, but not the sick knot in his gut. He had spent almost a month trying to adapt to the situation.

"We can't because something went wrong. Much like it was with superconductor research in the 80s, the application folks were way ahead of the theory people from the start. They'd encapsulate small weights and sent them back a few minutes. Somebody wanted to run a full proof of concept test. So, they sent a dog and a small vial of radioactive isotopes back 500 years. We found the vial, but no dog collar or bones. We guess the trip was successful and the mutt survived to take off for points unknown. Unfortunately, that test set up a shock wave."

"A what?" Launa growled.

"I need some coffee." What Jack really needed was time to construct his answer. They headed for the galley. He poured a cup while Launa knelt to rummage in the refrigerator, checking boxes of flight rations for what kind of sandwiches they held. Jack talked to her back.

"Nobody is quite sure what happened. One group swears the isotopes did it. Another thinks we need to refine the energy flow. Both agree that for now, the shock wave blocks any time between 1,000 A.D. and the present."

Launa groaned.

"Food selection that bad?"

"No, damn it." She glared up at him, agitation sharpening her voice. "Scientists shouldn't mickey mouse around with what they don't understand."

"Lieutenant, I've met them. They're good people. They've got a tough problem and some very important people think we need an answer real fast."

"That's stupid." Launa straightened up holding two ham sandwiches. "They ought to take their time and do it right." She handed one to Jack, grabbed a can of Diet 7-Up and followed him back to their seats.

As she belted in, Launa continued to storm.

"This time machine has already screwed up once. It could easily louse things up worse the next time. Do you really believe this pipe dream of a peaceful kingdom?"

She ripped into the cellophane wrapping her sandwich, stopped and looked across at him. "We could get back there and find a world totally different from what we've been told. On top of that, no one can tell us whether we'll be changing our time line or starting off on another tangent. If we go back 6,000 years, we would be changing everything. Mozart. George Washington."

She waved half a sandwich at him. "Good God, what are we risking? Hasn't anybody stopped to think about all that? I've just got into this thing and I can rattle off a half-dozen reasons to forget the whole idea."

Jack slowly nodded agreement. "I've raised every doubt you've named, and a few more."

"Well?"

"There's another card." Jack admitted, then paused to swallow hard.

Launa sat back, waiting for him to go on.

Jack rested his eyes on the land outside the plane's window. The patchwork quilt of farms seemed so orderly, so rational. Why was not the rest of the world? He turned back to her, his words heavy.

"The intelligence communities may not have penetrated the Movement, but that doesn't mean we don't hear some things. Outside Nairobi there's a big medical research lab. It was tied in with the global effort on the AIDS epidemic. Lately, the thrust of its research seems to have taken a new twist. We suspect someone is trying to modify the virus into an airborne strain. Some third hand Chinese intermediate range missiles may have recently been retrofitted to carry dispersal flasks instead of explosives."

All color drained from Launa's face. "Nobody's stupid enough to use biological agents. A fourth-year cadet knows you can't control dispersal or endurance. It's a weapon no sensible commander would touch."

"Unfortunately, the Movement is short on War College grads," Jack observed dryly. "They don't have professionals to do the staff work for a leader who doesn't want to hear that his idea is anything less than great."

Launa yanked her seat belt loose and shot from her chair. For a long minute, she paced the aisle like a great cat in a small cage. Suddenly she froze, then turned back to Jack. "I remember how big the Movement is on hating Europeans. One recurring theme in their propaganda is how our underfunding AIDS research was intentional genocide against Africa and, God, we never sent them enough drugs, even aspirin. Sweet Jesus," she exploded, "the logic of using AIDS as a weapon is there. But can't they see it's a dead end?"

The final question was not aimed at Jack, but to the world slipping away from them beneath the wing.

"Lieutenant, desperate people don't see the desperation in their actions."

"Yes," Launa's words were little more than a whisper as she slipped back into her seat. "An occupying army would have a docile population if the people were waiting for their next dose of medicine."

Jack nodded. "But if the release got out of control, it could finish everything that has ever been started. There are other contingencies. I keep holding onto that thought. We are only the last reserves -- the Forlorn Hope. We don't go unless there's nothing left to lose."

He offered her the life ring he had held onto this last month – the one thought that kept his own shock, fear, helplessness, and anger at bay.

Leaning back in his seat, he rested his eyes on the ceiling before giving voice to his thoughts. "Everything will have been lost already."

They sat in silence the rest of the flight to Jackson Hole, Wyoming, the sandwiches forgotten.

INTERLUDE 1

Bakuza Qwabes did not shiver as he approached the Leader this time. The heat of the day never reached where he worked in this vast building. He did not leave his desk before sunset and was always back as first light creased the sky. Two nights he had slept at his desk.

This was important work for the Leader and the people.

As Bakuza neared the Leader, he could not see the man upon whom the future of Africa and all its peoples hung. A ray of the sun pierced through the stained-glass windows above the nave. Its light enveloped the leader and dazzled Bakuza's eyes.

"You have word for me on what the Americans are doing?" The Leader's voice boomed from the light like a god from of old. Bakuza Qwabes fought the urge to fall to his knees.

"Yes, my Leader. We still do not know what the Americans are about, but we have information concerning a woman working on the project."

"Can she be trusted?"

"She does not know it yet, but she can be made to walk as we tell her."

"Very good."

4

Launa awoke, heart pounding, from a nightmare she could not remember. The phone was ringing. By the dim light of the clock, it was 0500 local time, she surveyed her surroundings. It took a moment to remember why she was not in her room at West Point – and never would be again.

She reached for the phone. "Yes?"

"O'Brian?" He sounded chipper for the hour.

"Yes, Captain."

"Want to join me out front for PT? Say in ten minutes?"

"I'll be there." The phone clicked from his end as she hung up.

Launa rolled out of bed and dressed quickly. She finished tying her jogging shoes with five minutes to spare. With luck, she would be half-way through her warm up before he got there.

As she closed her door, she turned to see Jack close his.

They exchanged silent waves.

Behind her, she heard two more doors click shut. Turning, she saw a man and a woman. Their t-shirts blazed with

Special Forces emblems, their camouflaged sweatpants rode above tightly laced combat boots. The man gave Launa an appraising once over. The woman, too, paused to study her.

Before Launa could respond, the two turned and strode to the back exit.

Launa joined Jack. As they went down the red tiled stairs she whispered, "Who are they?"

Jack made no answer as they hastened past the immense gray stone fireplace that towered from floor to beamed ceiling. The noise of breakfast preparations came from the dining wing.

Pushing the heavy oak front door open, Jack finally spoke. "They're Captains Dick Miller and Marilyn Brunner, Green Berets. Sometimes they're plan A, sometimes we're plan A. I don't know who's who this week."

Launa frowned. She had lulled herself to sleep last night counting, like sheep, the alternative ways out of this crisis – submission, diplomacy, compromise, bombers, commando raids. The list was endless. But if her group was committed, she wanted to be on the team to go. She knew a good plan allowed for redundancy, but she hated the idea of being second best.

As they crossed a stone veranda and parking lot she turned to Jack. "Should we check out with security?"

"I suspect they know where we are." Jack paused to look around. "When the ranch isn't busy like this, I understand it actually is a dude ranch and turns a profit. The electronic surveillance is so tight, and the cover so solid with the locals, that routine military security is unnecessary." Launa frowned and Jack continued. "I often think the 'purloined letter' approach more elegant than having guards running around with M-16's. I suspect if anything out of the ordinary happened, the easy-going ranch hands would be anything but."

He led her away from the stables and out-buildings to a dusty area between the parking lot and lush grass surrounding five large willows. Facing east, he started stretching his legs.

Launa wanted to ask more questions, but he did not seem disposed to answer. She joined him in the warm up. After a moment, he began talking, still looking east. "We're over 4,000 feet up. The air's a tad thin. I was at Schofield Barracks before here and about destroyed myself the first week trying to keep up my old pace. I've had time to adjust. I'll call the sets, but you might want to set your own pace."

Launa was on the verge of snapping that she could keep any pace he could, when the concerned undertone in his voice got through. She studied him for an instant. He continued his warm-ups, eyes fixed on the still dark horizon. She had met put-down artists in the Army and she had put them in their place, but Jack's suggestion seemed sincere. She had never been stationed this high and had no idea what to expect.

When they finished warming up, Jack turned north. "Let's start with running in place." He did not call cadence, but Launa could see him out of the corner of her eye and matched him step for step. By the time he called the switch to jumping jacks her lungs burned and her breath was coming in gasps.

With a wry shrug, she turned south and slowed her pace. Her competitiveness would never let her knowingly be out done. Jack was right.

He did not want to see her go slow and she could not watch him go fast.

When he called the next change, her blood was not

screaming for oxygen. She started to pick up the pace. Slowly, her body settled into a harmony of its own. Midway through the morning workout, the rhythm was solidly in place. This was fun. This was pleasure.

This worked the kinks out of the body and fear out of the mind.

When it came time for the final run in place, Jack turned back to her. "Feel up to six miles cross-country?"

"In beautiful country like this?"

"I missed my runs yesterday. So, if you don't mind, I'll take the shorter of the four trails."

"Go ahead. Take it easy on yourself." Launa would have laughed if she had the air.

First light painted the east. The clean morning air smelled of sagebrush and juniper. Birds called to each other. A pair of jack rabbits scurried out of their way.

"We're going to make a right," Jack called back fifteen minutes later. In a moment, she saw why. They jogged into a clearing.

The view was enough to take away what little breath she had.

The edge of the rim rock plunged five hundred feet to the valley floor. They trotted parallel. Just as the sun nudged its way above the mountains, Jack called a halt at the crest of a rise.

Launa's eyes swept to the horizon and every point of the compass. Gray rugged peaks soared to the west. The clear morning light etched every detail. The mountains to the east were still draped in soft shadows. The valley below showed in dazzling hues of gold, purple and green. The wooded plain they stood on rolled away from them.

Launa's eyes drowned in the beauty.

Jack turned slowly, easily catching his breath, a soft

smile on his lips. Launa wondered what went on behind that smile, those eyes. They watched together, breathing deeply as the colors passed from fairyland to merely spectacular.

Jack stretched, touched his toes. "Ready to head back?"

Launa trailed him. Who was this man? She had answered his questions. When would she learn something about him?

S howered and dressed in jeans and a flannel shirt, Launa joined Jack and headed for the dining room. The place was empty except for the two cooks. One of them, an elderly, round Mexican woman, met Jack with a big hug and a kiss. Stepping back, she laughed. "I've got two bowls of your breakfast special."

"Ah, Maria. I can always count on you and the sun."

"Oh!" She swatted him with her dishtowel, "Who is your friend?" Maria turned and Launa found herself greeted with a smile and arms that were as open as the sky.

"O'Brian, meet Maria. If ever there was a mother to nourish the world, it's Maria."

Maria engulfed Launa in a hug that left the Lieutenant disconcerted. Hugging had not been a thing to do where she grew up. Just one of Maria's caught Launa up on twenty-one years of missing.

Jack led Launa down the food line. Beside the boxes of dry cereal stood two large bowls filled with – something.

Jack took one. She picked up the second one like she might a snake and frowned at it.

"You'll like it, trust me." He picked up a large bowl of mixed fruit and pointed her toward the tables.

She chose a table in a corner by a window; they sat on opposite sides. Between them, the salt and pepper shakers supported a one-page news sheet. Launa made a note to read it. They took in the window's spectacular view of horses frisking in corrals, rolling plains and mountains.

Jack paused as he picked up his spoon. "I enjoyed working out with you this morning. I'd like to do it regularly."

Launa was not used to conversation like this before breakfast; her mind went blank. "I, uh, don't like running alone. I'd enjoy sharing your morning jog." That was not what she had meant to say; it sounded so impersonal. To cover her embarrassment, she pointed at the bowls before them.

"What's this?" She tried to reinforce her question with a funny face. She must have succeeded; Jack pushed back from the table with a laugh.

"It is not twigs and nuts. What people eat these days is so over-processed you have to read a label to know what it is. You and I have to get use to eating food raw, tasting the grains, roots, and berries the way nature meant them."

Launa gave the griddle a wistful look. "No more pancakes drowning in maple syrup?"

"You couldn't have drowned many and kept the figure you've got."

"I bet you say nice things like that to all the girls you're taking for a 6,000-year ride." There, that sounded better.

She looked around. "Will the others be joining us?"

Jack shook his head firmly. "Each team is pretty much freelancing. Their exercise usually goes twice as long as mine. If we're lucky, we'll have the place to ourselves."

Launa started to relax. Then, from the corner of her eye, she caught motion on the stairs. A woman in red descended into the great room. The sound of four inch heels tapping on the tiles reinforced the impression of self-assuredness and power.

The cut of her dress was enough to raise Launa's eyebrows. Where did some businesswomen find the tailored designs that came out so damn sexy? The full, mid-calf length skirt swirled with purpose and strength. Somehow, the cut between collar and waist managed to officially hide yet blatantly emphasize a pair of full breasts that any high school girl would kill for.

The woman stopped at the entrance, her eyes sweeping the room. She hardly noticed Launa, but her face lit with a predatory smile when she spotted Jack. "Jack Bear. You're back and you didn't tell me."

Her voice came out a grating soprano. Launa disliked high pitched voices, but this woman she hated. All her life, boys had forgotten she was in the room when one of these gorgeous, over-developed tanks swept in.

"Maria, a grapefruit and two pieces of dry toast today." The woman began issuing orders. "I'll be eating with Captain Bear and his little cadet."

With that, she moved on them with the pomp of a reigning monarch. "Oh, hell," Jack breathed as he got to his feet. Launa stood, as she might for a senior officer. Jack brought a chair and held it for the woman.

"Oh, you needn't have stood for me, honey. You must be Lora O'Brian, the cadet Jack brought back from West Point." She took the seat as he slid it beneath her. Jack got a kiss on the cheek for his effort.

He wore a pleasant, if stiff smile, as he sat down.

Launa struggled to keep her face neutral. She hated being called 'Honey.' Furthermore, she was a Second Lieutenant now.

And the woman had gotten her name wrong.

"I..." Launa started, but got cut off.

"Oh dear, I haven't introduced myself. I'm Samantha Tanner. You can call me Sam. I'm project manager for the Neolithic Task Group. I report directly to Robbie Prather, the Deputy Secretary of Defense for Research. He is personally overseeing this project, the boys at Livermore and RAND, and each time period's assigned groups. There are six teams like us getting ready."

Launa suspected this woman could talk non-stop all day.

"RAND? The RAND think tank?" Launa slipped in.

"Why, of course. Jack darling," Samantha put her hand on his arm, "didn't you brief this poor child on my project?"

Jack stopped a spoonful of Maria's special halfway to his mouth and glanced at Launa. "I sketched out the tactical situation for her."

"Oh, you strong silent men, always trying to out John Wayne each other. Well, I'll just have to fill her in on the big picture. The RAND Corporation has several of the world's biggest supercomputers working on this project. They've stuffed those poor dears full of every known historical fact. Not just the normal ones of who's doing what to whom, but the way-out stuff like the size of the polar ice caps and weather reports and things like that. They're running all this under some kind of program called self-organization or chaos theory. They want to find what I call cusp points. Places where civilization turned a corner. It's kind of like you and me, honey."

Launa saw Jack dig into his breakfast, finishing looked like the only escape. She took a nibble; Maria's special tasted quite good. She started shoveling it in.

Samantha kept right on talking.

"You get up every morning, put on your face, and go to

work. The same old drudgery every day. Then two guys want to marry you. One's a ball to be around, the life of the party, but you'll probably end up supporting the poor dear. The other's a solid citizen, money in the bank, the right connections, but baby, is he a bore. You'll be on your own for kicks. And once you make your choice, that's the freeway you drive until you come to another interchange. The boys at RAND say it's a long way between interchanges for civilization."

Maria brought a tray and sat it before Samantha. "Anything else, Ms. Tanner?"

"No, thank you. Oh Marie, if you have any of that delicious Kiwi fruit, I'd love two of them." Maria had not turned away. She seemed to expect the second request.

"I'll look in the refrigerator, Ma'am."

"Now, where was I?" Before Samantha could roar off in another direction, Launa decided to steer this Niagara of words toward something she was concerned about. "Can you tell me more about the other groups? Is one of them likely to go?"

"Oh, heavens no, child. One of my teams will be picked. The others have too low a chance of success. How could two people stop the fall of the Roman Empire? There are forty-four possible outcomes from intervention by my group and eighteen would be successful. All the other groups combined don't have half as many chances. No, I'll choose the team that goes."

Samantha positively glowed at the prospect.

"But really, this world situation will work itself out. We have the best people working on it. Several close friends of mine, in fact. I'm sure the Movement will be reasonable when given the right offer. All the African leaders I ever met were very reasonable men."

There was not much Launa liked about Samantha, but she liked that idea.

Maria's arrival with a bowl full of Kiwi fruit drew Samantha's attention. Jack took advantage of the distraction to pocket two pears and stand up.

"Launa and I have got to be running."

"Jack, darling, you're always running. Do come by my room sometime and rest your feet. I've got several things I'd like to talk over with you before I decide which team gets the final go ahead."

While Samantha's attention was on Jack, Launa picked up the whole bowl of fruit and headed for the door.

Maria gave her a knowing wink on the way out.

Once past the door, Jack made a beeline for the far end of the veranda. He stopped only when he was out of room.

"Who is that woman?" Launa blurted when she caught up.

Jack traded the pears for a banana. "She's the political appointee that someone made boss of this group. God only knows what we need with a political hack."

"She keeps saying 'my team', and 'my group'. Is she going with us?" "If she goes," Jack growled, "I don't. No way!"

He peeled his banana, took a bite and resumed in a calmer voice. "Don't worry; her idea of roughing it is carrying her own briefcase. She would never leave the halls of power; she loves possessing things too much. Here, she holds our souls in her carefully manicured hand. But where we're going," he clinched a fist and grinned, "it's our mission. I like that."

Launa had spent the night trying not to think about where and why they would be going. To avoid examining that too closely, she picked the first thing that came to mind. "What does she do around here then?"

"What needs to be done," Jack snorted. "She takes care of the budget and logistics. If we need anything, she makes it appear. She spends her day overseeing all kinds of exciting administrative junk that save us from wasting our time. I guess she earns her keep, but she does like twisting men around her little finger. I've got too stiff a backbone for that."

Launa found a wooden chair and sat. She put the bowl on a small table, picked a pear and bit into it. Juice sprayed.

Jack sat on the guard rail, munching his banana, his legs swinging back and forth.

"Yesterday, Lieutenant, you asked why we didn't just send an assassin. Would you take a one-way ticket to go back, rent a car, and run down a six-year-old kid on his way to school?"

Launa did not need long to find that answer. "That's not why I joined the Army. Couldn't the government find someone who does that?"

"Right, the Mafia has plenty, but there's a catch. Who do you get when you hire a murderer? Once he jumps, does he do what you paid him for? What else does he do?"

The two exchanged thoughtful nods.

"Soldiers hold the ancient civic trust. We're disciplined and loyal. After the jump, you and I are going to give new meaning to the word free agent. Better to send an ethical team."

Launa was getting plenty of food for thought. A Colonel's daughter learned early the Army was much more complex than civilians assumed. Still, what she'd been dragooned into was way past complex. She licked juice off her fingers and changed the topic.

"What's the drill today? Will we operate with the other team?"

"No. I've got an anthropologist and archeologist for you

to meet. You asked how much you can trust the historical data. These two can answer your questions if anybody can. Briefing starts at 0800. Shall we head over?"

Jack slipped off the rail and picked up the fruit with a chuckle.

"You did a neat job of walking off with the bowl. I didn't notice you hanging around to help Samantha get your name right."

"I'll straighten her out on several things next time I see her. Unless . . . " Launa grinned sideways at Jack. "What are my chances of dodging her for the rest of our stay?"

"A lot better than mine."

The two shared a laugh that tasted good in Launa's mouth.

AP Headlines for May 4, 1999

- BASEBALL SEASON STARTS AT LONG LAST:
  This Year's Strike Longest of the Last Three Years
- 2 MILLION PERUVIANS SUE U.S. AND DOW:
  Peru's Attorney General Joins Suit.
- RECENT REPORT SHOS BIRTH DEFECTS
  CONTINUE FROM COCA DEFOLIANT U.S.
  UNILATERALLY DROPPED DURING 1996
  OPERATION "SUDDEN SWOOP."
- INOCULATION FOR AIDS READY FOR
  HUMAN TESTS: French Doctors seek human
  guinea pigs in Africa; Governments Object
- SKIN CANCER UP 5% IN USA
- NIH BLAMES CONTINUING DEPLETION OF
  THE OZONE FOR 1998 INCREASE

- WORLD HEALTH ORGANIZATION REPORTS
- AFRICAN POPULATION DOWN 8% FOR 3RD YEAR; Deaths from AIDS Outstrip Births
- INSURANCE BAILOUT PROPOSED
- CRUMBLING REAL ESTATE MARKET IN CA AND JAPAN BLAMED FOR SHRINKING ASSETS.
- BABY BOOMERS' RETIREMENT FUNDS THREATENED
- And today, President Dave Lark took time off from his Budget Deficit negotiations with Congress to meet the Marigold Queen from Peoria, Ill.

5

J ack hoped Launa liked Judith and Brent. They had offered him an anchor of rationality and stability in this sea of endless "what ifs." Launa would be a good comrade in this forlorn hope, even if she was a bit idealistic. The more he saw of her, the more he liked.

His thoughts about her were changing, almost by the minute. A fear gnawed at him. Was he grasping for something lost? Launa was an enjoyable young woman, smart, capable, and a good officer. He would have to be careful to keep any other feelings on hold. He seemed to live most of his life on hold.

He got them to the meeting room a few minutes before 0800 so she would have time to get comfortable. The place looked more like a parlor than a conference room, with four comfortable chairs gathered around a small coffee table. But the casual atmosphere was off-set by the two eighty-inch flat monitors hanging on one wall and the recessed plugs built into the table to give network access.

While Launa drew aside the drapes and let daylight onto the knotty pine paneled walls, Jack checked the refrigerator.

There was plenty of ice and three Diet 7-Ups had been added to the usual assortment of soft drinks and juices.

At 0800 he heard the voices of the two specialists in the hall – as usual, they were arguing and only stopped as they entered the room.

Jack grinned as he introduced them. "Lieutenant Launa O'Brian, this is Professor Judith Lee." A short, middle aged woman took Launa's offered hand. She wore khaki slacks and a shirt that matched her snow-white hair.

Jack hoped Launa spotted the sparkle in Judith's green eyes.

"I'm Brent Simpson," a tall gray-haired man interjected. He sported plaid pants, a gray tweed sports coat, an outrageously colored bow tie and leather sandals over bright green socks. An unlit pipe was clenched in his teeth.

"Think of me as the loyal opposition. I'll drag up rumors and hearsay to refute the pipe dreams and suppositions Judith tries to sell you."

Launa gave the man a quizzical look as she sat, but Judith moved quickly to answer.

"What Doc Bulldozer means, is that we'll air our professional differences for you. You can decide for yourself who's right."

"Doc Bulldozer?" Jack had not heard that one before.

Brent waved his unlit pipe as if to ward of bugs. "The lady thinks I do my research with a bulldozer instead of a brush and dental pick."

"Well, you do." Judith sat, pulled a computer out of her tote and plugged it into a receptacle on the table.

"I did once." Brent leaned forward, pulled his computer out of a shoulder bag of brightly woven cotton, plugged it in, and faced off with Judith across from him. "There was good reason to take the first couple of layers off that old tel with a dozer. Life's too short to waste time on the recent crap."

"And getting shorter." Judith cut him off. She hit one key, her computer beeped and the screen on the right lit up.

"PEOPLE OF THE MID-NEOLITHIC AND HOW THEY LIVED"

Judith cleared her throat. "I hate dry lectures. If there's an English word, I'll use it.

"Good, then maybe we won't sleep through this."

Jack jerked his head toward the door. Captain Dick Miller came through it, followed closely by Samantha and Dick's partner, Marilyn Brunner. Even at this distance, he could tell that someone had not bothered showering after their morning workout.

Samantha took center stage. "Jack, I meant to tell you but you ran out so quickly after breakfast. Since Lora is getting a full briefing on the target time and these two haven't gotten one yet, I've ordered them to sit in on this. I'd stay myself," the administrator was already heading for the door, "but an old friend is passing through and we'll only have an hour of so between flight. He's quite insistent that I see him."

Two ranch hands with chairs made way as Samantha sailed out of the room.

Jack watched her go, wondering why she had fallen out of character. Normally, Samantha was quick to drop names, most of which Jack had never heard of and never wanted to meet. Why hadn't she dropped this name?

The ranch hands deposited their chairs where Dick and Marilyn pointed. The two captains did not join the immediate circle around the table, but sat off at a distance between Brent and Launa.

"We can move our chairs to let you in closer." Launa said, starting helpfully to slide hers toward Judith.

"No need," Marilyn waved a hand. "We don't want to upset the computer network and we can hear what we need to from here."

Judith smiled at the two new arrivals. "What would you like to know?"

"Oh, I don't know." Dick shrugged, looking around at the walls of the room. "We've read the briefing papers. We're trained to handle any situation. We figure we can handle this one."

"I could be of greater service if you could tell me what you think you need to know." Judith offered again.

The two green berets looked at each other, then stared at Judith.

"Well," Launa put in tentatively, "if you two don't have a question yet, I do."

All eyes turned to her.

She looked around and when the silence grew long, continued.

"What makes 6,000 years ago so important? In the last twenty-four hours, that date keeps coming up. Why?"

Judith sat back and took a deep breath. She frowned and let it out.

"Graves." Brent spoke the single word.

"Graves?" Marilyn raised an eyebrow.

"Actually, funerary gifts." Judith corrected them both. "Between 4200 and 4000 B.C.E., there was a radical change in what people in Southeastern Europe were buried with. Before that time, we found many burial sites. Nearly everyone has jewelry, tools, or cooking utensils. After the break, that detail changes. It's not easy to find a grave for the average woman. And the ones we do find . . ." She tapped her computer.

The screen showed skeletal remains. An ax, three spears,

a bow with a few arrows, and several bronze knives were apparent.

She hit the keyboard again. The picture changed to show a diagram of the grave. Judith rummaged in her tote and brought out a small flashlight. She pointed it at the screen and an arrow appeared. "This warrior was well provided for in his next life. Here rests his horse. This deer should feed him for a while. And to serve him, are these two women, four children, ages eight to ten and, at his feet, a teenage boy and girl. Quite an entourage, don't you think?"

"Could they have died together?" Launa asked slowly.

"Not very likely," Judith answered

"When I kick off, I hope everyone just curls up and dies right along with me," Dick chortled.

Jack grimaced. If people weren't careful, Dick might get his wish.

Brent frowned and tried to keep the meeting on topic. "In recorded time among the American natives, we have situations where the death of a chief triggered mass suicides among those who knew him."

"That's one way to avoid a complicated grief situation," Jack muttered, then turned away, immediately regretting his words.

Launa shot him a puzzled glance.

Brent ignored Jack, turning in his chair to face the two skeptics. "On one side of the break, people lived in towns of up to 5,000 people. The architecture is sophisticated, occasionally even including sewer systems." He played with his computer. Several strange things flashed on his monitor. Finally, a town map filled the screen.

"At last," he muttered. "People lived in single family dwellings of about twenty-five square meters. Religious shrines were plentiful and distributed evenly." He looked at the group. "Let's see how long it takes me to find my next AV."

"I think I can help you." Judith hit two keys and her screen lit up with a map. "Notice that after the break, the houses are half dug-outs, of about twelve square meters. This is an architecture that was common thousands of years earlier. That's where the common folk lived." She hit another key.

Two large rectangular halls appeared, surrounded by a palisade.

"The building on the right served a cultic purpose. The one on the left was the chief's. This fort was built on a hill. Ladies and gentlemen, meet your first two-bit dictator. He's brought a thriving economy to its knees, but who cares, he's the boss."

Judith looked like she had bit into something sour.

"Well, now I know where I want to live?" Dick nudged Marilyn.

"The basic idea is to make sure one person doesn't live like that while everyone else has nothing." Judith sat up, ramrod straight. Her voice had a hardness Jack expected in a general officer, but it surprised him coming from the diminutive scholar.

"Before 4200 B.C.E., in Europe, Western Asia, and Egypt, a culture thrived that concentrated its efforts on increasing production and creativity. Its people lived in partnership, treating each other as equals. It was replaced by a culture that concentrated on tools of destruction and established a domi-nator/dominated relationship. Human beings became tools.

The anthropologist paused to let her words sink in.

"That earlier culture deserved to survive; it was better than its replacement culture by any measuring stick you choose to use. Both your teams are tasked to protect these people so they can thrive and grow. This would change civilization for the better."

Launa nodded; Marilyn pushed herself out of her chair to pace the room. She halted to peer at the pictures on the monitors, then turned to Judith.

"All this talk about graves and architecture is not helping me. Our mission objective will never put us in contact with these people. However, while we're on the subject, it takes a war to advance technology. Without a little fighting, this culture is going nowhere."

Judith held her ground. "Look at what they did. Between 6,000 and 4000 B.C.E., they discovered farming and domesticated animals, made cloth from flax and wool," Judith ticked them off on her fingers, "and created pottery. They began trading and ship building. Art advanced outside the cave. We have the beginning of the symbols that led to writing."

Judith's exasperation clearly showed.

"Hell, without the ravages of war and dark ages, they probably would have been writing before 3,000 B.C.E. I can't prove they would have kept progressing, but they had a damn good track record."

Launa interjected a question. "What type of political structure did the old culture have?"

Jack gave her another check mark. A good leader knew when to switch off of a hot issue and cool down a meeting.

"That's a tough one," Judith leaned toward Launa. "They left no documents, but as late as 3,000 B.C.E., records mention cities ruled in the 'old way,' by a council of elders under a Queen. These elders were both women, and men and came from all lines of work."

"What about the Queen?" That had gotten Marilyn's attention.

"Don't think of her as a female king. The accounts allude to kingship coming down from heaven to settle on a ruler about 2700 B.C.E. The idea of one-man rule is a recent innovation. I'd say the queen functioned more as the center for consensus."

Marilyn laughed. "Sounds like a pretty dull job to me, assuming it works. In my book, you need a strong leader if you expect to get anything done."

Now she turned to Dick. "I haven't heard anything here that wasn't in the brief and that I didn't pick up in a fourth-year history class. We'll just hang loose and prepare for anything. To me that means spending time sharpening individual skills, not sitting on my duff. Let's go, Dick."

"Right."

In a moment, the two were gone, leaving nothing behind but Jack's frown. He had never considered anything from Samantha an order, but he never would have walked out on a briefing.

Who was in charge here?

This lash-up had been thrown together too quickly. What with the CIA, civil service, scholars, and soldiers, the chain of command was a total knot. Which one of the captains was senior officer present? Did it matter? If he was, how would Dick or Marilyn react?

Unbidden, snippets of M*A*S*H came to mind. And under it all was his stepfather's voice, "Boy, you've got to make things happen. You can't wander through life like some drunk Indian."

Launa was talking. Jack decided to let his memories ride and turned his attention back to the briefing.

"I didn't want to raise this in front of those two, but we

are planning the most important invasion since Normandy. I don't feel very comfortable with phrases like, 'the records mention', or a thousand years after the fact 'the accounts allude to'. All you're giving us are crumpled burial piles and stories written years later by those who did not survive, written by those who did."

"I'm sorry, Lieutenant," Brent offered in a concerned voice. "It does appear our best intelligence is a trifle stale."

Launa's head snapped back to Brent. She turned to Jack just as he lost his struggle to keep a straight face. The tension broke as both soldiers collapsed into laughter at the absurdity of the situation.

The scholars looked at the two young soldiers, then at each other, and joined in.

"I've never thought of archeology as military intelligence." Judith finally got out.

"I've never thought of military as intelligent." Brent fired back giving Jack and Launa a sly sidewise look. "Present company excepted, of course."

"Why bother with an exception?" Launa laughed. "We were dumb enough to volunteer for this, weren't we? That wasn't too intelligent."

To Jack, this sounded like a good time for a break. If these puns got any worse, someone might get hurt. "Would anybody like some coffee or something to drink?"

The meeting dissolved as the four poured beverages.

Brent stepped out on the balcony and was lighting his pipe when the others joined him. For several minutes, he and Judith reminisced about the digs of their youth. When they fell silent, Launa brought them back to the present.

"What is that other team's mission profile?"

Jack grimaced and Brent stepped in. "They're to ferment

civil war among the horse raiders. That would buy the Old Europeans more time before the invasion."

"But they'd still get hit." Judith added sourly.

"Could we send both teams?"

"Not likely." Jack shook his head. "The machine is weight-limited. They want to take horses and I can't blame them. Drop them on foot in the middle of the steppe and they could die of thirst before they found water. Besides, our drop zone is west of the Danube. They want to be far to the east of the Dnieper. No one is sure there will be time to attempt a second drop once the first team is inserted."

Launa shook her head as if to clear it. "God, this stuff is hard to think about. Part of me expects to wake up in the Infirmary at the Point and find it was all just a fevered nightmare. Another part is scared stiff we're overlooking something, like when we'll get there and need a can opener."

Brent nodded. "I know how you feel."

"Our problem is to plan ahead so these folks can make the rescue with their pants on," Judith sprouted an impish grin. "Assuming the Neoliths wore anything. Have I shown you my dirty pictures?"

Jack felt warmth rush to his face. It had not been that way the first time Judith showed what they might be wearing. With Launa at his elbow, it was different.

He headed back in. Slowly, the three followed him.

When they sat back down, Jack turned to Brent. "What do you see as downside risks to us?"

"How about the queen grabbing you for her lover and you getting your gizzard cut out for New Year?"

"Hold it," Judith protested. "That's not a likely risk."

"What do you mean, would Jack get chopped up?" Launa voiced Jack's concern faster than he could.

Brent looked defiantly at Judith.

Judith breathed a deep sigh. "This comes under the heading of Those Who Win, Write the Histories. The male dominated histories say some female-led systems used to sacrifice the queen's consort every year. The economics of this system defeat me. I should think they would run through their supply of available consorts rather quickly."

"Yeah," Jack observed dryly. "Like the first year."

"There is no hard evidence for this practice," Judith said. "I can't say the same for the dead women in the conqueror's tombs."

Brent would not back off. "In Denmark, they've dug up well-preserved bodies of men hung as offerings to the goddess."

"Not fair." Judith said firmly. "They died in the first century B.C.E. By that time, the religious practices of the Goddess had been subjected to extensive adaptation, or perversion, by the male-dominated gods of the invaders."

Jack jumped in. "Could we take a time-out for us poor soldiers to clear our heads? Lieutenant, any comments?"

"Yeah. I sure hope State can come up with something else. This whole idea is beyond crazy," Launa said.

Judith and Brent chuckled.

Jack nodded; he knew how she felt. He didn't want to think about how he'd handle an execute order – probably shit his pants. "Well, let's take a look at our tactical problem. Brent, can I have a closer look at that bow in the grave? If it's a simple short bow, it won't have a range better than fifty meters. If it's a composite, it's good to 300 plus."

Brent's screen lit up with the requested grave scene.

Jack walked over to look at the bow closely, his arms folded across his chest. Launa joined him.

"Can you get me a better picture?" Jack spoke without

turning away from the picture. "I can't tell from this shot if it's composite or not."

"No." Suddenly Brent looked very uncomfortable.

"Why not?" Jack immediately regretted the sharpness of his tone. His take-charge demon was slipping its leash.

Brent ran a worried hand through what was left of his hair. "Four universities participated in this dig. The manifest detailing who got what has been lost. I've searched all four inventories. None record having a bow from this time."

Brent winced. "It may be in a box that has never been opened and inventoried."

"Western civilization hangs by a thread, literally a bow string, and you tell me what the earth hid for 6,000 years is lost in some university storeroom?" The sharpness in Launa's voice surprised Jack. The Lieutenant was not afraid to snap at her seniors. He had better remember that.

Judith came to Brent's defense. "We're comfortable with computers, but some of our colleagues came late to these gizmos. It's not easy tracking all the artifacts turned up in the last century. Didn't you ever see that old movie where they take the Ark of the Covenant and lose it in a warehouse?"

Jack and Launa nodded.

"Well, it can happen."

That was how the morning went. Launa or Jack raised questions about social structures, access to metals, food surpluses, and other concerns of potential tactical value. Judith and Brent explained what they knew, why they did not know more, or shrugged and offered three answers, any one of which might be possible.

By 10:30 AM, Jack had all he could take. He suggested a run might help them control their stress level. Launa went, shaking her head doubtfully.

6

B rent and Judith lunched on Crab Louis with a French Chablis.

Jack ordered lentil soup, fresh corn tortillas, black beans, and water for himself and Launa. It was tasty, but Launa wondered at the need to give up civilized food so quickly and with such enthusiasm.

Jack refused to give ground. "They picked me for this mission because my Apache grandfather and the Army taught me to survive in the boonies. Mornings, we plan for the mission. In the afternoon, you're back in class, Lieutenant. I'll teach you how to stay alive."

"Yes, sir." Launa let her face go blank. She considered herself damn good at basic survival and had not expected to be treated like a tenderfoot. Still, she'd met brass before who felt their authority made them god of the world. Maybe she needed to modify her assessment of this one.

Conversation at the lunch table became awkward.

Finished eating, Jack pushed his chair back. "I think I'll change. I'd like to get some sun this afternoon."

"What have you put on the schedule, Captain?"

"I'm introducing you to the bow." Jack's tone left no room for opposition.

Launa hesitated, then opened her mouth. Before she could get a word out, Jack squelched her. "I'm your instructor in the afternoons, Lieutenant."

Slapped down, Launa folded her napkin and watched him leave.

"This'll be a short archery practice," she muttered to herself.

"Archery *practice*?" Judith's eyes twinkled.

"Some superiors have to learn the hard way, don't you think?"

Judith fought to suppress a grin, then gave up and laughed. "Oh, yes I do. That's one man who has a lot to learn about the job he's taken on."

Launa appropriated an apple from the serving line and munched it in the shade of the veranda. A few minutes later, Jack appeared wearing gym shorts and a t-shirt, carrying two long bows and quivers.

As they walked past the willow trees, he took off his shirt and hung it from the waist of his shorts. The muscles of his arms and shoulders showed firm under his lightly tanned skin. The overhead sun cast shadows on his flat belly.

Launa had seen solid in physique at the Point, but something about Jack went beyond just a well-formed body. The way he held himself as he walked stirred something inside her. He moved like a beautiful, wary cat, ready in a moment to hunt or be hunted. For an instant, she wanted to put her admiration into words, but only for a moment.

This cat had shown he had claws. She had to do something about his domineering ways quickly, before this animal decided he was king of the jungle.

Judith's lecture from the morning flitted across Launa's mind. How would an Old European handle this situation?

Launa snorted to herself. *They wouldn't have had turkeys like Jack to handle.*

Dick and Marilyn thundered by on two magnificent Arabians, his midnight black, hers a milky white. Both carried AR-15's slung over their shoulders. A rocker launcher hung from Marilyn's saddle.

Launa frowned. "Why are they practicing with that junk? They'll shoot themselves dry in a week."

Jack just shook his head.

Two man-size targets stood in the field beyond the willows. Jack closed to fifty meters and stopped. He handed her a leather wrist guard and demonstrated how to put it on.

She silently followed his lead.

"You hold the bow here, with your left hand." He instructed. "I prefer to notch the arrow when I have the bow horizontal to the ground."

Again, she imitated. Quietly, she slipped around him until she was a little behind and facing the right- hand target.

"You pull the arrow back carefully." He did it slowly. "You'll want to keep the bowstring away from your, uh, chest. Level the arrow at the target. Raise your aim to adjust for the time of flight, and let go."

As he released the arrow, the bow string gave a satisfying 'twang'.

Launa had already nocked her arrow. As he shot, she aimed and let fly.

He must have felt the shaft whiz by his ear. He turned, a startled look on his face.

Just as quickly, he spun back to the targets as two

'thunks' told him arrows had hit the target. He studied them.

Launa defied anyone to tell which struck closer to the dead center of the bull's-eye.

When he turned back, Launa wore her best 'cat who ate the canary' grin, and said, "Thank you for your introduction to the bow, Captain."

She added a curtsy to her sarcasm.

"Obviously, you two have met."

"At summer camp when I was twelve." Launa kept her words dry enough to burn.

"Why the hell didn't you tell me?"

"You didn't let the Lieutenant get a word in."

Jack handed her a quiver. "How good are you?"

"Good." Launa stayed noncommittal. He had to learn.

"We'll see." Jack paced off more distance. She followed. He stopped at double the range.

She talked as she nocked her arrow and slowly took aim. "In Bushido, it doesn't matter so much whether you hit the target, as how well you draw the bow."

Jack took aim as slowly as she; they let fly together. Their eyes followed the shafts until they planted themselves firmly in the target next to the first pair.

Jack shook his head and grinned. "I know when I've been had. What else have you been holding out on me?"

She started pacing off more distance. "I continued archery through high school, also fencing. I could have lettered in both. Neither high school I went to had teams, so I lettered in field, track, and soccer."

"Soccer?"

"Yep. When I was eight, mom wanted me to take ballet. The Colonel wanted me to start soccer. The Colonel's lady said I needed poise and balance. The Colonel said I needed to learn teamwork and how to win or lose."

She shrugged. "Mainly win."

"Who won?"

"I took ballet." She went up on point, gracefully pirouetted beside him and, coming to an abrupt halt, kicked for his knee cap.

Jack dodged.

"And played soccer. Whenever the Colonel and his lady had a disagreement, that's how they solved it. Not either or, but both, and."

She stopped after another hundred meters. Both their shots landed in the bull's-eye. This time, they exchanged proud grins.

"Shall we try three hundred?" He asked.

"Why not? If the English archers could do it at Agincourt, so can we." Launa said as they started to walk. "I'm good at pugil-sticks. I figure quarterstaffs ought to be a pretty effective weapon against short swords."

Jack thought for a few paces. "Good idea. We might try the Zulu short spear for heavy infantry. Your pike idea is good, but we need a reserve to handle any bad guys who get in among the pikes."

"I agree." She quoted rule one. "No battle plan survives contact with the enemy.' Axes or maces would fit with the time."

"Right," Jack agreed, "but the axes were stone. I wouldn't want to count on one against even leather body armor. There weren't many copper axes."

"Why not bronze? For God's sake, the other crew's carrying rifles. Why are we arguing copper verses bronze?"

Jack nodded. "Because somebody thinks that at least one

of these teams ought to look like they belong where we're going."

Then he scowled. "Unfortunately, our advisors can't agree when the breakthrough to the Bronze Age occurred."

"Judith and Brent aren't sure?"

"They're good, Launa, but you and I are going to have to live with a lot of unknowns."

"That's okay by me, Jack." She spoke his given name for the first time. It tasted good in her mouth. A brief smile flitted across his face. Was the sound as pleasant to his ear?

"This looks like three hundred meters to me." Launa turned back to targets that were now tiny. "Shall we take three shots?"

Jack nodded and nocked an arrow. Three shots later, Launa had one more arrow in the bull than Jack, thanks to a last second change in the wind.

"Archery is like life, a crap shoot." Jack shrugged.

Launa laughed. It felt good to be alive, to be here, to be doing this with Jack. "It's a wonderful game, if you can laugh when you lose."

Jack started at her words. "That's not always easy," he murmured softly, but his body had changed. His shoulders seemed rigid, held higher. Silently, he picked up his quiver and began to tramp back toward the targets.

Launa retrieved hers and ran to catch up. As she joined him, Jack began talking as if nothing had happened. "It's tough at this distance. The wind can get you when you're hanging an arrow in the sky for six seconds."

"What about a moving target?"

"The French were nice enough to give the Brits massed knights as targets at Agincourt and Crecy. Even at this distance, you just loft an arrow toward them and it was bound to hit something. I doubt the horse raiders will have that many troops on one field. But, we shouldn't have to judge deflection shots. They'll be coming straight at us."

They chuckled at their questionable good fortune.

Jack stopped to unstring his bow. Launa took care of her own. "I had planned to spend the next two hours teaching you archery, then turn you loose for a break while I looked over our horses. You ride, don't you?"

"Does driving a Mustang since I was sixteen count?"

Jack laughed, then shook his head. "Not really."

"Hey, I was going Airborne. I skydive. In case you haven't heard, cavalry rides helicopters these days."

"But we won't. I guess I'll have to teach you to ride."

Jack teaching her to ride was low on Launa's list. "No, you're not. The Colonel couldn't teach me to drive and you're not going to teach me to ride."

Jack took a step back and scowled. "I don't follow the logic there."

"Well, for me it's there. You go look at your horses. Find someone that teaches dudes how to get on the right end of one. I'll start this afternoon. Right now, I'd like to take that break I earned."

For a moment Jack worried his lower lip, then he nodded. "Okay, we'll do it your way."

In the shade of the great room, Launa realized how thirsty she was; her swim could wait for iced tea. As she filled her glass, she spotted Judith and Maria at a table in the corner. The scholar waved her over.

"Hi. How was introduction to the bow?"

"Short. I beat the teacher." Both women shared her laugh.

Launa took a seat beside them. "Now I'm taking a break, though Jack seems to think life's too short to relax."

In their situation, Launa saw some relevancy to that attitude, but she was not sure she could ask Judith a question in front of Maria.

Judith must have sensed her reserve. "We can talk with Maria. I don't think anything goes on here that Maria doesn't know about."

Maria smiled, but said nothing.

"Well," Launa scratched the back of her neck, "the Kurgans spent several hundred years attacking the Europeans. What was the life expectancy then?"

"It averaged about thirty-five years, but some lived into their seventies. You're young enough to lead the defenses you and Jack build for a long time."

"Oh, now I see why you wanted a kid on this project," Launa said.

"Don't sell yourself short. You've got a good grasp on the problem; to create a defensive capability without creating a warrior dominated society. It's a tough job, but, Launa, it isn't your job alone. We're hoping you and Jack can give the Old Europeans the edge in a rematch, but remember that you're dealing with creative people. They'll have their own ideas. Some of them will surprise you."

Launa sat back in her chair. "Primitive doesn't mean stupid."

Maria nodded. "You may be the best woman for this mission."

After watching Marilyn today, Launa was not so sure.

"You speak German, Japanese, and Arabic." Judith pointed out.

Launa shrugged the praise off. "The Colonel was overseas a lot."

"Yet," Judith pressed on, "many Americans never go off base."

"True, but I was fascinated with the places and people around us. I loved to bike around Germany when I was old enough. Even Saudi wasn't too bad as long as I stayed covered up."

"And you were willing to stay covered up?"

"Yes."

Judith shook her head. "You still don't see what you bring to this project other than your youth, do you?"

Launa grinned sardonically. Now that the excitement was wearing off, she was starting to realize the competition here was as tough as any at the Point.

Do I have what it will take?

Judith leaned forward in her chair. "I've known Admiral Benson, Chairman of the Joint Chiefs, since we were kids. A few years back, he was waiting for housing at a new posting and I offered him and his lovely wife the hospitality of my home. One evening, I shared my latest research. He's always had a taste for history."

Launa nodded, waiting.

"Last month, he asked if I still thought the middle neolith was special. When I said yes, he offered me this chance to do something about it."

Faith, and maybe a hint of the zealot's madness, shone in Judith's green eyes.

"There are a dozen teams getting ready. Each has two of the toughest, meanest, green beanies the United States has, just like the pair we've got here."

Launa grinned; Judith had picked up the Green Beret's nickname.

"But that wasn't what I wanted for my team, and the Admiral let me set the parameters. I'm sure you could give any one of them a run for their money in a fight, but I wanted more than just an iron fist like we saw this morning. You're not locked into a mind-set. You'll examine all the solutions that come your way, even the silly or unorthodox."

"What does that make Jack -- my keeper?" Launa did not like the idea of being the local *Infanta* even with a *duenna* as good looking as Jack.

"No." Judith shot back, then paused before continuing. "Jack's a combat veteran, but he's paid a lot of other dues as well. You'll find him a good example of late twentieth century man, with all their vision and misperceptions. There's more to that man than you expect."

Launa wanted to ask what that was. She was beginning to get glimpses into her superior. How did his slip about grief fit into his reaction during archery about loss?

Damn it, why can't a junior have a look in her boss's personnel folder?

"What are you going to do about Jack?" Maria asked. Launa realized the two women across the table were looking at her with one of those strange smiles that older women give unmarried ones.

Launa tugged at her shirt decisively. "I'm going to teach one pig-headed man that women have got the vote."

That ought to keep those two off her case for a while, maybe long enough for Launa to figure out what she really wanted to do with one distractingly appealing, if confusing, captain.

Judith gave her a crooked grin. "Well, it might be just as well to let nature take its course. Have you plans for the afternoon?"

"I want to get in a swim, then I'm being introduced to a horse."

"Introduced?" Maria echoed.

"Yeah. I got the right to miss a few things in my career planning."

They laughed as Launa got up to leave. Judith called after her, "Want to join Brent and me for supper?"

"You bet."

T he Colonel and his Lady held definite opinions about what their daughter should wear. The tiny two-piece swimsuit in Launa's dresser would have brought on apoplexy for those two and got her thrown out of any base pool she had ever been at. Still, the tag said she could tan through it. That might save her from having to explain tan lines to some neolith if her future uniforms were as skimpy as Judith kept hinting at.

If Launa had not found the pool all to herself, she still might have chickened out. Once she dove in, the feel of the water through her skimpy suit was unsettlingly pleasurable. The water caressed her breasts and abdomen bared by the suit. The swim left her breathless beyond mere exercise.

One mile later, she pulled herself from the pool. She had just laid down on a lounger to catch her breath when Marilyn sat down in the chair next to her.

"You swam those laps pretty fast. You're in good shape."

"Thank you," Launa basked in the other woman's approval.

"For a minute there, you startled me. You looked so much like Sandy."

"Sandy?"

"Yeah, Jack's wife. I only saw her once, before I shipped out for some TDY in Africa. She and their baby died in a car crash while I was gone. Jack was pretty shaken up after that.

I thought we might lose him. He's really looking good these last few days, isn't he?"

"I guess so."

"Well, a girl can't sit around in a man's world. I better be running. See you around."

Launa watched Marilyn go, still trying to catch her breath.

She could not have been more blown away if Marilyn had used a rocket launcher on her. Jack had been married? He had a baby.

Secondary explosions went off in her skull. Was this what Judith had meant by Jack's dues? Launa looked like his dead wife; did that explain Jack's behavior toward her? She was damned if she was going to let Jack treat her as anything but a soldier.

INTERLUDE 2

B akuza Qwabes scanned the dispatch from America, then read it slowly three times, trying to comprehend its full meaning. It did not come easy.

A frequent problem with field reports was that the writers wanted to please the readers, or at least not draw down their anger. It was clear to Bakuza that the writer of this report did not want anyone to accuse him of believing what he was reporting.

If Bakuza understood the dispatch, the Americans were prepared to tamper with the very fabric of time in order to defeat the Leader. Frowning, Bakuza put the report aside.

He had been supervising the drawing down of the Stalkers in America. They were needed in North Africa. The Chief of Missions, United States, had beamed with pride as he explained his recruitment strategy -- "acquire information, but not operatives. This month's glowing recruit might be tomorrow's double agent. The stalkers in America are clean and lean."

They were also few and getting fewer.

A glance at his notes confirmed only seven teams

remained in America. The woman identified seven groups and a primary target. Assuming she was cooperating, Bakuza prepared a short note for the Leader. They had suborned the woman and would verify her information. For the moment, no further transfers should be made from America.

It was a good plan. It would be hard for anyone to fault it.

7

A t the stables, a laconic cowboy was waiting. Launa quickly went through the basics. After an hour, she headed for supper and a showdown.

They were ordering when Jack came in. As he took the last chair at their table, Launa took a deep breath and put down her menu. "Jack, we've got a problem. I'll eat your 'local rations' for breakfast and lunch, but the cooks here can match any chef in New York. I think we ought to enjoy supper."

"Am I facing mutiny already?" Jack studied Launa, then turned to Judith. "How would the Old Europeans approach this?"

"They'd listen to the woman." Judith snapped her menu shut.

Jack pushed his chair back. "Yes, they would. In fact, they'd be more likely to listen to the woman than to me."

Judith gave Jack that smile teachers save for a slow student who is finally catching on. Launa realized she had opened a bigger can of worms than she had intended.

The Captain pursed his lips. "Okay, I see the point. Where we're going, women may call the shots and Launa may be in command."

Launa had not expected Jack to give so much ground. She blanched, "I can do the talking, but that doesn't mean I have to command."

In her dreams Launa was the general, but not now. Not until she had some experience and had some time to make mistakes with a good sergeant and C.O. to back her up.

In her profession, mistakes killed people.

Jack shook his head. "Doesn't work that way. We're going up against some hard cases. You can't be looking over your shoulder, wondering if I'll support you. If women call the plays, you take charge and I follow. It's time I start working on that."

Jack faced Judith. "The Old Europeans built their culture on cooperation, right?" The scholar nodded and Jack turned back to Launa.

"Lieutenant, the normal chain of command isn't going to work. Everything I've seen about you so far makes me glad we're sharing this job. You and I can work as partners. If I forget that, give me a nudge. I'll do the same for you."

Launa studied him. After what Marilyn had told her, she did not know what to make of this man. He was full of surprises. What made him tick?

For the moment, she would take him at face value until she knew more about him. "You've got yourself a deal, partner."

She ran a hand along the edge of the menu. "There's still a lot I've got to learn. We'll work on that together."

"I suspect," Judith added dryly, "you both have a lot to learn. Now, can we order some food?"

Launa agreed wholeheartedly with both sentiments as she selected from the best the chef had to offer. Jack ordered the same, but skipped the wine.

During the meal, Brent kept up a running account of student pranks and professorial follies. He provided such detail that Launa began to wonder if he was quite the innocent bystander he claimed.

Late in the meal, Samantha joined them. She frowned when she saw Jack seated at a full table. Marilyn whispered something to Dick, who waved at Samantha from their table. The boss woman beamed and joined them.

Marilyn threw Launa a knowing smirk as Dick held a chair for the administrator.

"Just who decides which team will go?" Launa tried to keep the worry from her voice. Judith followed Launa's eyes to the other table.

"The computer will have a lot to say," Judith's green eyes were sober. "The Chairman of the Joint Chiefs will also. Of course, the President will have the final decision. Though I suspect Samantha thinks she will make it."

"She won't," Brent growled.

"I hope not," Launa added under her breath; then suppressed a laugh. Jack had spoken in unison with her.

"I bet you two didn't know that I am quite the horseman." Under Brent's urging, the four departed for an evening ride.

In the saddle, the old scholar's assertion proved to be a bit overblown. With this group, Launa admitted she had spent time with horses at summer camps.

"What more are you holding back on me?" Jack asked, only half laughing. Launa felt herself coloring. "I didn't want to look bad in front of you."

Judith gave her a wink. Brent picked that moment to challenge Jack to a race. Brent led off in a cloud of dust, but Jack quickly passed him, forcing Brent to give up the chase.

An hour later, Launa groaned as she dismounted. "I'm supposed to be in good shape, but God, I hurt."

"It's the jacuzzi for all of us." Judith sounded as definite as any mother.

Launa considered the swimsuit problem and almost backed out, but she was sore and she could not think of a more supportive environment to get used to being nearly naked around Jack.

Five minutes later, she was at the jacuzzi, shedding her sweatsuit. When Jack's sweats came off, his swimsuit was as tiny as hers. There was enough light to answer one question; Jack had not been circumcised.

They both splashed hurriedly into what cover the water offered.

The jacuzzi soothed Launa's complaining muscles. She was soon ready to call it an evening, but after fifteen minutes of quiet soaking, Jack sat up.

"What do we need to do to get ready?"

"I need to get out of this hot water." Judith pulled herself up, sat on the side, dangling her feet in the water. "Launa, what do you think you need?"

Launa also wanted out, but she was not about to sit around as bare as this in front of Jack. She prepared to soak as long as he. "I don't know how to weave or make clothes from skins. Do you, Jack?"

He shook his head.

Judith reached in her bag for pen and paper and started taking notes. "That's something you'll both need to know. I don't think they had separated things out into women's and men's work yet."

For the next half hour, Jack and Launa built a list. The scholars took notes and added items. It was Jack who finally suggested they get dressed and continue the discussion in Judith's room.

Launa was glad for the change. Was it her imagination or was Jack becoming as physically aware of her as she was of him?

The brainstorming session with Judith and Brent lasted until almost 2300 hours.

Jack shook his head as they finished. "Samantha's going to go crazy finding some of this. Security won't like all the people we want to bring in."

Launa bristled. "I'm not going 6,000 years from the nearest drug store without knowing something about herbal medicine, or a lot of other things."

Jack waved a calming hand. "We'll make them happen. Now, more importantly, 0500 is going to come early; let's sleep in tomorrow."

Brought back to the present, Launa gave him a grateful assent.

Launa slept until 0600. It worked out better. She needed the sleep, and Samantha was leaving the dining room at 0730.

The woman glared at Jack and ignored Launa. They joined Brent and Judith who were digging into pancakes and eggs. Launa found she really enjoyed Maria's 'special breakfast'.

Vocabulary was the morning's program, and it earned them a visit from the other team. "You didn't tell us you knew something about their language," Dick growled.

"You didn't ask," Judith said, not giving an inch.

Launa liked the iron in the woman scholar's backbone.

Brent interjected himself. "What we have are written examples of several conquerors' tongues. Quite a few words seem to have been borrowed. Words for plow, loom and the like, were grafted into the language."

"They stole the skills and the words," Judith growled.

"How's Jack supposed to say 'To arms, to arms, the red coats are coming'?" Marilyn grinned slyly.

"I haven't the foggiest." Brent missed the joke. "Verbs like 'to be' and 'to come' were already in the invaders' tongue. They didn't borrow them. But the real problem is finding someone damn fool enough to take up arms."

Jack looked straight at Marilyn. "Seems to me, the Civil War was the last time people had guts enough to face an enemy who wanted to jab sharp steel in their gut. Then there's the second half of the problem. Mom shared how my father felt when someone spat on him after his first Vietnam tour. Grandfather wondered what he got for fighting Japanese in the Pacific. Why fight?"

"The son of a Congressional Medal of Honor winner couldn't be going pacifist on us now, could he, Captain?" Dick jabbed.

"Posthumous medals make you think." Jack's face went hard as he turned to the professors. "Would non-violence get to first base with the Kurgans?"

"I think that's what the Old Europeans tried." Judith reached out to rest a hand on Jack's arm.

"We won't have any problems like that," Dick crowed. "A bullet at long range for the headman, and we're in charge. After that, anyone who crosses us is dog meat."

"Right on!" Marilyn gave him five.

Brent kept doggedly to the topic. "It will be hard to

persuade a Neolithic farmer to take up arms. To raise an army, you'll need to think like them; things like rhetoric and argument in the classical sense. That's why I'm here."

"So, think like an ignorant gook," Jack replied.

"You're kidding?" Dick shot to his feet and stomped for the door. Brent's eyes followed him, resting on Jack's face.

"You need to quit shaving," Brent noted.

Jack looked startled. "You're right."

Dick stopped in the doorway.

With their attention captured and refocused, Brent continued. "You also have to quit speaking from the mindset of a twentieth century man. These people are not dumb. They're different. Let me show you."

Brent fiddled with his computer for a few seconds, then the screen lit up. Two women dressed in flowing gowns stood on either side of a nude man. He held a plow by its yoke pole.

"Found it the first time." Brent congratulated himself. "This shows the Goddess giving man the plow."

"Two women are there." Jack observed.

"Right, they're different manifestations of the same Goddess." Brent continued. "Note his penis." It was draped across the pole.

Dick chortled. "It's bent weird. If that's the way they all are, the women will be glad I came."

"Oh," Launa frowned thoughtfully at the computer screen. "The angle of his penis and the angle of the plow shear are the same."

"You got it." Brent rewarded her with a grin. "These folks know nothing about the science of biology, but they know if you plow the ground, it's more fertile."

"And if you plow the women, they are too." Judith

continued. "Their handle on cause and effect is not tied to scientific proof, but they know how the world works."

Jack was beginning to see the full extent of his problem. "So, to simply say 'the Kurgan is the enemy' is too twentieth century. It's too vague for the Old European by its very exactness. But, if I say the Kurgan is a river in flood, destroying all before it, they could see my point?"

"That's it." Judith beamed. "Let your Indian blood speak."

Jack shook his head, feeling inadequate to the praise. "Remember, this Indian did most of his growing up in L.A."

"But, I still see a problem." Launa spoke slowly, as if struggling with the question. "The flood is a natural part of the world. The Goddess sends it for good and bad, and you just have to accept it. If the Kurgan's are like a flood, won't they think of them the same way?"

Brent and Judith nodded slowly.

Marilyn got up. "If you people can't give us better stuff than this, we've got better things to do."

Jack walked over to the window and let out a long breath as the door closed behind them. "When I first got here, I wanted to 'kick the tire, light the fire, let's jump tomorrow'. I settled in to wait, because an infantryman has to be patient. I'm beginning to see that we need time to put this show together."

Launa nodded. "We've got a lot to learn and it's not just how to make bows."

Most of that morning, they studied words and the way they might be pronounced. Just before they left for their run, Brent began introducing the soldiers to the rudiments of allegory.

Jack and Launa spent the afternoon at the metal shop learning to cast copper and bronze.

Launa left Jack bent over a mold when it was time for her riding lesson.

L auna knew the other team was competition, but she had been raised that soldiers were supposed to be comrades. There was no excuse for not pulling together.

Always before, Launa had been able to find a way to patch up people's differences. Even when the colonel was drunk and the folks were going at it, she had usually found some middle ground for them. Not the last time, of course, but usually.

She did not like the way the two Green Berets kept hitting it off wrong with her and Jack. When she spotted Marilyn coming from the stables, Launa decided it was time to do something about it. "Marilyn, you got a second?"

The woman turned and waited.

Launa got straight to the point; from the way Marilyn held herself, patience was not her strong suit. "Would you and Dick like to join Jack and I for supper tonight?"

"You eating with those two school teachers again, Lieutenant?"

"Usually, we do. We're picking their brains for all they're worth."

"Why bother?" Marilyn snorted. "Lieutenant, you don't know how to play the game. They'll drop Dick and I with high powered rifles and a couple of good horses. We'll be running a horse clan inside a week and have them killing each other in a month." The woman grinned at the thought. "The gooks 'll tear themselves up so bad it 'll take 'em four hundred years to find their asses."

Launa had never met such a cold-blooded person. Her nose felt the tingle of frostbite. *She's got to be kidding.*

But Marilyn was still talking. "Six thousand years later what we do will still strike fear in people's hearts. No son of a bitch will ever use me again. I'll have the power then. Marilyn the Terrible. I kind of like the sound of that. Hell, I could take my horsemen south and conqueror the Euphrates valley. It'd be fun being the first Empress of Babylon." Marilyn scoured the sky, seeing more than Wyoming.

"Back then, a woman could take what she deserved, not settle for the tame shit they hand out now." She turned and swaggered off.

"She is for real," Launa whispered under her breath. Who had hurt this woman so much that all she wanted now was to hurt the world first?

"I'll pass on supper," Marilyn called over her shoulder.

Launa was glad. Comrades or not, she had enough of both of them.

That day set the pattern for the next two weeks; Special Forces went their own way. Launa and Jack spent the mornings exercising the body and the mind. Launa picked up what language possibilities she could. Both found there was nothing sloppy about thinking in allegory and metaphor.

They had to be just as exact as any scientist searching for the mythical thirteenth decimal place. During one warm up, Jack admitted that learning from Brent was like drinking from a fire hydrant.

Launa pounded him on the back for the metaphor.

Afternoons were technical. They learned to work wood

with fire, stone, and bronze tools. One afternoon, they went bow hunting for elk and Launa dressed out her kill. The next day's lesson was on the natural tanning processes for that hide.

In the following week, they learned to make needles from bone, threads from sinews, and clothes from hide. Surprisingly, most of the instructors they needed were already on the ranch staff. Her instructor in making wool yarn was a strapping six foot four computer geek.

Launa did not ask where the computers were.

Growing up Army, Launa had never been much of an animal person. With so many family moves, she had never had so much as a pet goldfish. When Jack took her behind the barn and introduced her to three huge dogs, Launa almost jumped out of her skin.

The sweet collie, Mist, she could handle. Frieda, the German shepherd, looked like she wanted to take Launa's arm off, and almost did, under the watchful eye of the trainer who showed the dog's attack skills. But it was Alert who almost drove Launa around the bend.

A cross between a great Dane and some Viking's castle, the dog was immense and constantly living up to her name, searching everywhere, eyeing everything, and chasing anything.

In one afternoon, the trainers poured as much information into the two soldiers as time allowed, even showing them how to use Frieda on a search. Launa got over the worst of her terror. Jack made it clear that he considered the dogs a critical part of the team, but Launa wondered if either of them knew enough to get one tenth out of the dogs that they had to offer.

Launa enjoyed the time she spent with Judith and Maria. She knew she was trying to gather a lifetime of wisdom from these two women who had lived such different lives from each other and the one Launa had planned for herself. Yet, they both seemed to have a peace about them. The one thing she did not do was quiz them on Jack. As much as she wanted to know more about him, it did not seem honorable to pump his friends behind his back.

O ne of Launa's most memorable afternoons was with Maria. The cook took Launa in an old pick-up truck to several plant reserves. As they walked across a field, Maria pointed out a plant that softened the pain of child-birth. She pulled a root from the ground and offered it to Launa to taste. When it was sweet, it was food. When bitter, it was good for controlling fever.

Maria was a walking encyclopedia of plants. She shared with pride that her daughter was finishing a Ph.D. thesis on the medicinal properties of prairie vegetation. Launa suspected the daughter got more of her knowledge from home than lectures and libraries.

Launa ended the afternoon shaking her head.

"I can tell ninety-five different armored fighting vehicles at a glance and identify most combat aircraft from any aspect. But both times I took survival training, the instructors just told us to watch what the animals ate and eat small portions until you knew it was okay. Beyond naming a rose or a lily or a dandelion, I don't know a thing about plants."

Maria pulled the truck over to the side of the road. "Child, how could you live so long and know so little?"

"I grew up Army. All I had to know about trees was not to run my tank into one. Bushes were for camouflage. Food came from rations or McDonalds. Medicine was what you got from the first aid kit or at sick call." Launa shrugged. "I thought I was pretty well prepared to survive."

Maria shook her head. "We must help you. My daughter has a book that is very old and has many pictures. It has much to say to you. You can study it and maybe take it with you." Maria smiled knowingly.

Launa nodded; there was so much to learn and so little time, yet it was fun and exciting. Here, people shared what they knew without pressure or expectations. These were good days.

Even when some unconfirmed and vague rumor caused the alert status to go up a notch and the ranch hands to wear side arms, Launa hardly spared a moment from her thirst for learning.

AP headlines for May 25, 1999

- INSURANCE BAILOUT HEARINGS TODAY: Slide in Real Estate Market Raises Price Past Three Trillion
- MAJOR BREAKTHROUGH ON AIDS: New Wonder Drug takes on all Viruses; Doctors Expect to use it on Everything From Cancer to the Common Cold. Years of Testing Still Required
- QUIET MAN CHARGED IN GREEN RIVER MURDERS: Clues found on 247th Victim's Body Lead Police to Make Arrest
- RIOTS BREAK OUT IN CHINA: Young Couples Protest "No Child" Tax
- FOREIGN MINISTERS TO MEET IN NAIROBI: US and EURO Ministers to Meet with African

Ministers Trade and Foreign Aid to be on the Table
- DEBATE ON OLD GROWTH CONTINUES DESPITE SPOTTED OWL EXTINCTION: Barred Owl Did It, Government Scientists Report. It's Just Nature's Way, says Interior Secretary

8

J ack was sitting down to breakfast when the Communication Tech appeared at his elbow. With her close-cropped hair, ramrod back, and muscled shoulders, the tech was probably the only person on the ranch who looked the Agency type.

The message was directed to Samantha first, Jack second.

Samantha was sleeping in late. Dick had introduced her to western dancing and she had acquired a Stetson, boots, and tight jeans. Their nights were spent in town; she rarely breakfasted before eight o'clock. At least now, Jack did not have to hide like a buck on the opening day of hunting season every time he saw her.

Jack read the message through slowly, initialed the form, and returned the clipboard to the tech. She came to attention, gave him a quick nod, and left.

He turned to the others. "We are in a two-week stand-down," he said.

"What's that mean?" Launa asked.

"Admiral Benson says to assume the mission will not be

activated while they're making a major effort to resolve things diplomatically. I imagine the cowpokes should be turning in their guns."

"I'm old enough to remember Pearl Harbor." Brent frowned.

Judith handed Jack the day's AP news brief. "There isn't much here about Africa. Did the Admiral tell you more?"

Jack glanced at the three cryptic lines. "France and Chad arranged a summit of foreign ministers through the old Organization for African Unity. With the Movement so shadowy, there's no formal machinery for folks to approach it. The OAU has been pretty moribund, but it's a recognized institution where people can talk. At the economic summit last week, the Big Seven settled on a package of trade and economic aid they think will defuse the African problem."

Jack sliced a pear while the others thought.

When Judith raised her juice tumbler, four glasses clinked to her toast, "To peace in our time."

Brent grimaced. Jack wondered if she intended the full ambiguity of Chamberlain's boast after Munich.

The meaning was not lost on Launa; her tight smile showed full understanding.

Despite the stand-down order, they adjourned to their conference room right on schedule. Brent led off the session with a discourse on the finer points of Roman logic as exemplified by Cicero's arguments against Cato.

Jack had trouble keeping his mind on the lecture. He had always assumed a C-5 circling the local airport might be their first notice to pack up and go. Now that he had two weeks to plan, he began thinking how to make the best use of the time.

Equipment was fine. No one knew if he should be taking bronze or copper woodworking tools, but he had a good set of both. The ponies met his specs, not award winners, but the most durable. The dogs were a good combination and highly trained. Now, it was he and Launa who fed them, played with them, and ran with them. Unlike the stallions, the dogs were all bitches, and two were already pregnant.

There was only one concern left.

Launa.

She did everything well, of course, but she had never operated without a safety net. Marilyn's casual remark about Launa's youth and inexperience kept nagging at him. What if he died and she was on her own? God knows that was possible. Launa needed a confidence building experience. She needed to spend time in the woods on her own.

Yes, that would do it.

Another part of his brain told him this was all bullshit.

He was the problem, not Launa. He was the one who hated the thought of her alone in a primitive and hostile world. His "hero" pedestal was getting attractive again, the quiet voice warned him.

He had a defense against his scolding self.

If the time came where she was separated or on her own, she needed this experience to draw on, to boost her confidence in herself. This was a reasonable extension of her mission preparation. Jack was sure of that.

He just wished his stomach had not gone so sour.

During the break, he excused himself and made a phone call.

After the morning session ended, he and Launa dressed for a work out. When she came out of her room, he beckoned her.

"I want to check the horses. Got a minute?"

She smiled and went along with him.

At the corral, he whistled to three quarter horses. Despite the heat wave, the ponies left their shade and trotted to him at his call.

As Windrider and Big Red took the sugar cubes he had brought, Launa fed an apple to Star, the chestnut she had chosen.

"Why not Percherons? Marilyn has one."

"Have you ever tried riding one of those monsters? They're a real pain in the ass. Besides, this little paint reminds me of the horse my grandfather gave me the summer I turned thirteen." He stroked the muzzle of his pony, then turned to her.

"Grandfather took me on a three-day ride. We ended up at the sweetest spring right in the middle of the desert. It must be the only swimming hole in the state of Arizona." He leaned on the corral. Launa's face showed keen interest in his story.

"I'm swimming around, cool for the first time in a week, just having a ball like any kid, when I look up and there's my grandfather. He's on his pony, with my clothes slung across my horse, leading it off. I screamed 'Grandfather!' He hollered back, 'The house is a three day walk that a way'." Jack pointed to the east with his entire hand, not just one finger, as his grandfather had done.

Launa listened, one foot resting on the lower rail. Jack had not seen her so attentive since the plane flight out. This was going easier than he expected.

"By the time I got out, grandfather was long gone. I started walking. For the next three days, I ate roots, bugs, and a couple of lizards. I scooped water out of cactus. Even flaking out under a bush during the worst of the mid-day sun, I made it back in the three days he gave me. Exhausted and sunburned as hell, I walked in the house, went straight for the kitchen sink and drank a gallon of water. Grandfather kept right on watching I Love Lucy."

Jack settled back against the rail. Launa smiled. Grandfather's taste in television had not sounded Indian to Jack in those days either.

"After I got dressed, he took me into town and bought me a Coke and a rifle. That was when he taught me to shoot. He said if I could take care of myself on the desert, I could take care of a gun."

At that moment, an old Huey flew over. It was low and the savvy pilot had used the barn to mask its approach. It landed in the open area next to the corrals. Jack motioned Launa to it, then ran for the open door.

She followed, frowning. Once aboard, they buckled in and Jack waved to the pilot to take off. He had already told him where to land.

Launa leaned over and shouted. "What's up?"

The UH1D always had been a noisy bird; this old buzzard was no exception. Jack hollered. "Wait until we're back on the ground, okay?"

Launa grimaced and sat back in her seat, her face a mass of storm clouds.

Thirty minutes later, the chopper settled into a small clearing next to a rock-strewn brook.

Jack got out, moving at a crouch until he was away from the rotor blades, then walked quickly to the banks of the stream. Launa followed.

With the helicopter engine at idle, they could talk.

Jack turned to Launa. "You need a confidence building experience. A good survival hike will show you what you've got. That will be a big help after we make our jump." He made sure to keep the confidence in his voice.

Launa's eyes narrowed to slits. Her hands clenched into fists that landed on her hips. "Captain, I have better things do with my time than wasting it running around the boonies. I know this stuff. I don't need to prove it to myself, you, or anybody."

Jack swallowed. He had stated his case. He had taken the high ground. He did not have to defend it.

That he could not defend it only made it worse.

Launa scowled and began to redden. "I'm not a thirteen-year-old. I know my shit."

Jack folded his arms across his chest, set his face like flint and shook his head firmly. "Lieutenant, this mission depends on every fiber of your body knowing you know this stuff. You need this practice run."

***

Launa felt her face flush. Jack had been flakey all morning. When he opened up about his grandfather, she had hoped he was finally going to let her in.

Well, look where that little chat led.

Taking two steps back, she folded her arms across her chest and let her face go to stone. "God damn it to hell, you're pulling this Captain - Lieutenant crap on me again. You said we wouldn't do that."

Shit, she was cussing like a trooper. She hated when she did that.

ack said nothing, just did his imitation of a rock.

Like the colonel, he had spoken. Like hell she would put up with this. A rock could be out maneuvered. She whirled and stalked toward the Huey.

Jack grabbed her by the shoulder and spun her around. Her fighting instincts took hold. She barely pulled the punch she aimed at his gut.

His right froze inches away from her left.

For the moment they stood stock still, glaring at each other.

Launa raced through her options. He would not let her back to the chopper without a fight. If the two of them went hand to hand, it would not matter who won, the mission was lost. As so often with the colonel, logic left her one option – do it his way.

She relaxed out of her fighting stance, took a step back and stood to her full five foot four inches of height.

"God damn you, you pig-headed, macho son-of-a-bitch. You can do this to me, Captain. But you're fucking up and you know you're fucking up."

She stomped past him toward the stream. His face stayed hard as iron as she passed.

"Lieutenant, I'll trouble you for your sandals."

Launa whirled back to face him. "Shit! Didn't your grandfather leave you your boots?" She waited for Jack to answer, but he was giving an Oscar winning performance as a clam.

"God damn it, Jack. We're taking sandals with us. I'm not going to be left barefoot and pregnant."

Now what Freudian slip made her say something stupid like that. It did not matter. Jack said nothing.

"Hell! Damn! Shit!" As she stooped to take off her sandals, her anger went from red hot to white hot to glacial cold.

She stood up and threw her sandals at his feet.

"Your grandfather left you bare-ass naked didn't he?"

Again, Jack said nothing. Did his jaw drop a fraction of an inch?

In one fluid motion, Launa stripped off her shorts and top and threw them down beside her sandals. Naked, defiant, defenseless, she faced him.

Jack stooped to collect her clothing. When he stood up again, they stood as armies arrayed for battle. Smoldering eyes glared from stony battlements that had been faces.

Jack spoke, emotionless, into the silence.

"Fifty miles downstream is an abandoned cabin. We'll leave a transmitter under the porch. Call us for pick up when you get there."

Now it was Launa's turn to refuse any reaction.

Jack gave her an almost imperceptible nod, turned and walked the distance to the chopper. Strapping himself in, he looked back at her. Their gazes locked.

Defiant, she put her hands on her hips, refusing to hide her nakedness from his eyes.

Without taking his eyes from her, he signaled the pilot. The Huey rose into the air and quickly disappeared over the tree tops.

Launa watched the helicopter go, eyes blinking rapidly. The rotors kicked up a lot of dust; the rule book said to look away. Damn the rule book.

Damn his eyes.

He better have liked what he saw. Probably did, he had seen it before. Damn him and his dead wife.

Damn her eyes. Between the dirt and anger, she was about to start crying like a baby. Why in the name of all that's good, holy, and military, did she have to cry when she got emotional?

She did not mind crying when she was happy, but, shit,

why cry when you're mad? She rubbed her arms, restoring warmth, while considering what to do next.

"He's gone, you're here. Now clean up your language, clean up your act, and get this show on the road."

That was the logical side of her talking. It had gotten her marooned here.

"Shit, shit, shit, shit, shit, shit," she screamed at the mountains.

That was the emotional side of her that had gotten her into this assignment without a moment's reflection.

"Why didn't that idiot listen when I told him I did jungle survival in Panama when I was fifteen and desert survival in Bahrain when I was seventeen? Talking to Jack is like talking to the Colonel."

Launa stomped toward the brook, then froze as her mind went over their argument. She had said she knew her stuff, but she had not told him why.

"Damn!" Her temper had done it to her again. Jack must have been checking her personnel folder. Of course, paperwork isn't kept when an army brat sneaks through a program. Her explorer status was enough leverage to make it possible, but no one put it in the Army records.

Jack had jumped to the wrong conclusion on her again and she had gotten mad and forgotten how to communicate, again. "Damn!"

Then she laughed; it came out a solid belly laugh. "Well, girl, if you can laugh at yourself, you'll live."

She took a deep breath; the scent of pines and water came with it. She looked around her. "Not a bad place to work."

Carefully, she trod the stones to the brook, knelt to wash her face and took a drink. The water looked clean, but she knew that could be deceiving. They would get gamma glob-ulin shots before they jumped; they had not yet.

"Didn't think about that, oh all-knowing one, did you?" The words she aimed at the departed chopper dripped sarcasm as water dribbled down her chin.

She started downstream, thinking as she went. Food, shelter, clothing were the priorities. She could do without food for five days, according to the book. Why in hell couldn't Jack have waited until after lunch for this damn fool stunt?

Her stomach rumbled; she was hungry.

The stream meandered through a shallow valley with steep mountains rising on either side. It was warm in the shade of the pines now, but nights would be cold. Warmth was her first priority.

A geologist had shown them how to start a fire with flint and a rock rich in iron pyrite. She searched the stream bed for signs of either and ended up stepping on a sharp stone.

"Shit!" No blood, it just hurt. She stood in the sun as she analyzed her problem. Standard Army tactics called for one squad to advance while another provided covering fire.

She would watch where she was going while moving to a new observation point, then stand to study the stream bed. This would slow her, but not nearly as much as a badly cut foot or a broken leg. An hour of this provided her a hand sized piece of granite, richly speckled with fool's gold. As far as she was concerned, it was worth more than the real stuff.

An hour later the sun was sinking toward the mountain tops when she spotted what looked like flint. Stepping into the stream, she crouched and began feeling among the rocks for the dark stone.

Sun light sparkled on the water. The wind blew soft and warm on her skin. The sighing of the trees as the wind jostled them mixed with birds calls. Smells of earth, water and warmth assailed her. The dry lectures of Old Europeans feeling one with nature flooded her, taking on form and substance.

She was living them.

Her hands found what she had been looking for, a hard, sharp-edged black rock. Next to it lay two more. Retrieving all three, she stepped gingerly from the water. As she tested her finds, sparks flew. Now all she needed was some dry moss.

She started moving down stream in earnest.

When the sun sank below the mountains, the warmth of the day gave way to a soft coolness. These were the hours Launa loved the most – normally.

Bare to the air, she wondered how long her affection for this time of the day would last. She started thinking about making camp.

A fully equipped trooper could have pushed on for another hour. Now she knew why ancient armies settled for ten or twelve miles a day. Making camp meant starting from scratch.

She spotted a fallen log that offered good shelter. Through the trees was a clearing. As a kid at Fort Lewis, she had loved parks in the evening when rabbits sneaked into clearings to browse. Was there a rabbit tonight willing to accept her invitation to dinner?

How to persuade cousin rabbit to give itself over to her needs? Launa smiled at the way her thoughts slipped into the mindset of a Neolithic hunter. The rabbit was not a Big Mac to be ordered on drive through. It was a creature to be sought, praised, and thanked.

Okay, Launa's logical mind interjected, how do we seek it?

She had no sling. Throwing rocks did not sound all that effective. How about a snare? Some of the grasses and shrubs looked like the types Maria had shown her how to braid into twine and rope.

She set the rocks and moss down beside her deadfall, collected what she hoped were the right materials, and started twisting it. In an hour, she had what looked like three passable snares. She headed for the clearing.

There was plenty of grass for the rabbits. She located a slight depression down wind and laid her snares along runs in front of it. Settling in, she prayed for patience, rabbits, and that her stomach rumblings would not scare off dinner.

Thirty minutes later, her first snare broke and a rather cute little bunny departed for points unknown with half of her noose draped around its shoulder.

Twenty minutes later, its cousin was not so lucky. The next trap held just long enough for Launa to get her hands on a hind leg and swiftly snap its neck.

Collecting her third trap, Launa headed home for supper.

The fire was harder to start than she expected, but as light failed, her dinner roasted on a spit. She scoured the area for firewood and edible roots. Fluffing her bed of pine needles, she added a coverlet of ferns.

All in all, she told herself as she settled down to munch cousin rabbit, she had done well.

The sharper flint skinned the rabbit reasonably clean. In the morning, she would cut it into strips and see what kind of sling she could make. With luck, she would knock off tomorrow's supper rather than wait patiently for it.

As she snuggled into her den, the fire's embers casting warmth but little smoke into her nook, she heard the thump

thump of a helicopter. It could be any transient. Then again, it could be someone checking on her.

By all rights, she should let the son of a bitch stew in his own juices. Still, her temper bore part of the blame for her situation. She took a hand of pine needles and tossed them on the coals. They caught, burned brightly, then flared away to nothing.

Launa pulled her hand back under the fern cover, hugging her body's warmth to herself. She had done her good deed for the day.

Overhead, Jack saw the flare and waved the pilot to take them back. He had caught holy hell from Judith and Brent for what he had done. Officially, this trip was to assuage their concern. He had known that Launa would do just fine. Now that she had a fire, they would relax.

And so could he.

All afternoon, he stewed over what he would do if Launa got in trouble. God damn it, why had that woman thrown her clothes at him as well as her sandals?

Why had he asked for her sandals in the first place? This whole drill was not coming down as one of his better ideas. Launa was right. He was wrong. It was that simple.

He fidgeted in his harness. How could he back out of this gracefully?

Jack tossed and turned most of the night. Wherever Launa was sleeping, he hoped she was doing it more soundly than he.

INTERLUDE 3

Each time Bakuza Qwabes approached the Leader, it was easier. Each time he left the presence of the Leader he felt more empowered, as if breathing the very air around the Leader was a drug that strengthened his muscles, made him walk bolder, more sure of himself.

Bakuza crossed the marbled floor quickly, enjoying the decisive sound of his clicking heels as they reverberated around the chamber.

The Leader looked up. "You have more word for me on the Americans."

"Yes, my Leader. They are so bold as to think they can make time flow in a trench they will dig for it. We will show them differently. The woman shares our belief that the Europeans must atone for what they have done. Her report has been corroborated." Bakuza Qwabes allowed himself a grin.

The Leader rewarded him with a smile.

"The woman told us the location of seven other targets. We have assigned teams to attack them. She is prepared to strike at her own group, however something unexpected has arisen and she needs assistance."

"Send a warrior to her aid." The words were clipped, decisive, as if what they said was already so.

"Our best warriors are in the north, preparing to lead the people into Europe, My Leader. We have few assets left in America."

"There are enough killers in America. Hire one." The Leader snarled, then began to smile. "You have done well my son. For a woman who attempts to run in the warrior's race, she has done well also."

The Leader paused. A frown began at the tip of his lips, then deepened and spread as he spoke softly, as if to himself. "These Europeans and Americans have no limits to their pride and arrogance. What might they do?"

For a moment Bakuza Qwabes stood transfixed as the Leader stared through him.

The Leader burst from his chair, saying, "Come with me."

Bakuza had to run every third step to keep up with the pace the Leader set. Qwabes had never seen him standing. Only now did he realize how tall and broad-shouldered the Leader was.

In a moment, they were through a rear entrance. The Leader snapped his fingers; a black Mercedes materialized before them with a squeal of brakes. Bakuza opened the door for the Leader, then joined him on the back seat.

"Drive." The Leader barely whispered the command. The driver accelerated with a force that drew Bakuza deep into the leather seats. In a moment, they were past the basilica and shooting down the wide road that now carried pilgrims of a different kind.

They were barely out of the inner compound when the

car shook. Bakuza craned his neck to look back. The immense building disintegrated in a gigantic explosion. Huge slabs of marble and granite flew through the air. Chunks of stone rained on the speeding car like hail.

Bakuza turned in awe to his Leader. How had he known?

The Leader did not look back, but grinned, his eyes fixed straight ahead. "Did they think they could kill me so easily? My destiny is not to be thwarted by little men. We will go to Nairobi and I will face them down myself."

As an afterthought, he turned to Bakuza Qwabes.

"Order our agents to destroy the American teams immediately."

9

L auna awoke as the sun peeked over the mountains to the east of her. She stretched and shivered. It was cold.

Tossing some pine needles on the embers of last night's fire, she was rewarded in a few minutes with smoke. Judicious huffing and puffing gave her fire. Huddled around it for warmth, she munched roots left over from supper.

With the edge taken off her hunger, she quickly refashioned the snares into a pouch and belt to carry her flint, iron, moss, and a few dried bones that would serve as needles. With the sharper of the flints, she cut the rabbit skin into lengths. Tying them together gave her what she hoped would be a usable sling.

As the sun began to warm the morning, she headed downstream.

She picked up a pebble to test her new weaponry - and paused. In the dirt beside the stone were fresh cougar tracks. She had slept through company last night.

A trooper in the field, or Marilyn, might carry enough firepower to kill a herd of elephants. This running around bare-assed was dangerous. Her temper flared at the bastard who dumped her out here and she twirled her sling with enthusiasm, seeing Jack's face in her target bush.

She released at the wrong moment and the stone hit near a pine tree behind her.

"Damn that man!" She picked up another rock and began breathing exercises to calm her racing heart. She was not taking an assault rifle with her; she had better get used to facing claw and fang with her own two hands.

She missed the next target by a dozen feet.

She picked up a couple of rocks and added them to her pouch. The knots holding her sling together were coming undone. She tightened them. After several more shots, none of which got within several feet of the target, she was about ready to include this sling in the next disarmament treaty. It was nothing like the one she had made from elk hide.

She spotted a large level rock and stopped to scrape more fur off the skin. "We'll see if it holds together better than Jack's promises do."

Satisfied, she twirled the sling and nearly bounced the next rock off her skull. "Got to keep your mind on business, girl, when you're carrying a loaded weapon," she quoted the range master who had taught her to shoot at thirteen.

Every time she thought of Jack, she did something stupid. Next shot, she whirled the sling well above her head. The rock landed within inches of the sapling she had targeted – much better.

By the time she called a halt that evening, she was confident of her skills. In fifteen minutes, she nailed two large rabbits. The rabbit grease felt good as she massaged it into the sun-dried skin of her shoulders and arms.

She studied the skins as she waited for dinner. Sore feet won out over modesty. She began sewing a miserable-looking pair of moccasins using the dried bones of yesterday's supper for needles.

She felt a rising sense of confidence as she settled into her nest of leaves and ferns that night.

Again, she heard a chopper in the distance and turned her dying fire into a brief beacon. Let Jack measure the distance she had covered today. Tomorrow, she would cover a lot of ground and maybe reach the shack.

J udith walked with Jack to the waiting helicopter. The Captain nervously swung his helmet and Judith gave him a gentle pat. "Don't worry, she's okay."

"I'm not worried about her out there. It's what she'll have to say to me tomorrow when I pick her up that's scary."

Judith could not suppress a sharp laugh. "You're right, boy. You do have something to worry about."

They were interrupted as a cowhand raced up to them. "We got some hot dope coming in on the net, as well as CNN. Somebody just blew up a church in Africa."

Jack halted. "Church? Africa?"

Judith fingered a message flimsy in her pocket. It was not often that a civilian got personal message traffic from the Chair of the Joint Chiefs.

Take care, old girl. Something is about to happen. You may be at the center of it.

"Oh damn, the Leader's using a church for his chancellery," Judith said putting the pieces together.

"Yeah. They call it that too," the messenger said with a shrug.

"God, the fat's in the fire now," Jack said and dashed for the chopper.

He leaned in the window and shouted over the noise. "Something's come up. This may be a while. You better cut your motor."

Judith kept at Jack's elbow as he trotted after the CIA man to the com center. The helicopter rotors slowly wound down.

Which left her wondering, *What else is coming down?*

The com center was getting classified information from around the world. Nonetheless, a large screen in the front of the room showed Cable Network News. For once, even they were having problems following a story. Central Africa was not a hot news spot and their nearest reporter was in Tunis. For now, they were having to make do with the "official" news releases.

Hundreds were reported dead. The whereabouts of the Leader was not mentioned.

"Who the hell did it?" Jack asked no one in particular.

"Nobody's claiming credit. If they didn't get him, nobody's going to either," the gray-haired station manager said with a shrug. A veteran of Laos and too many points in between, the man had Judith's respect.

After a few minutes of being inundated with noise but no news, the CIA chief got down to business.

"We need to get everybody back on base and stand by for new orders. Samantha and Dick went to town an hour ago."

"I know Dick's haunts," Marilyn said, arriving in normal breath and not winded by her run to the center. "Give me a rig and I'll have them back in a half hour."

The chief tossed her keys. "Make it an hour. We don't want to lose anyone on the road."

Marilyn caught the keys one-handed and was gone.

"What about Launa?" Only the corners of Jack's eyes showed the tension that underlay the question.

The station chief turned to stare out the window at the deepening dusk. "It's a half hour flight out to where you left her."

"Yes."

The old spook shook his head. "These birds are ancient and none of my folks are qualified for any of that fancy night flying shit. We're going to have to pass on that, son. You can get her at first light," said the old warrior, trying to soften his command.

Jack nodded, shoulders drooping.

Judith looked away. She did not believe in kicking a dog when it was down and there was no way Jack could miss what she felt.

Judith had met few young women whose heart could see as far as Launa. She belonged here, not at risk out there.

Jack left.

Judith went looking for Brent. She had no time to waste agonizing over what might-have-been. The two of them better prioritize what was left to be done. They might not have much time left.

For the next three hours, snippets of news were passed from the com center as they came in. Rioting broke out in several African cities, but Nairobi was not one of them.

Near midnight, the station chief called them together. "Okay, boys and girls, nothing's happening and you're losing sleep. If something comes up, you're going to miss that beauty rest. I'm doubling the watch here. If anything breaks, we'll be the first to know. Now, I'm going to bed. I suggest you do the same."

Launa slept well and came awake at first light. The fire was far gone. She did not try to bring it back to life; the day would get hot soon enough. Grabbing her gear, she slipped into her make-shift moccasins and started south, letting the fast pace warm her.

With luck, she would make the pick-up point by mid-afternoon.

She noticed it almost immediately; the woods were quieter. She had gotten used to the small sounds of the forest. Insects always made some noise, so did birds. Launa thought she could hear the steps of deer as they passed through brush.

She was hearing none of those this morning.

On a whim she stopped, knelt, put every fiber of her being into listening. She heard something – then again. Then nothing.

Picking up a rock, she ambled on. Someone was following her. Jack?

Not likely, his wood skills were better than that. Casually she put the rock in her sling and shot at a tree. It bounced off. *Make it look like practice, girl.*

She stooped again.

Whoever it was following her quickly stopped this time, but not fast enough.

She picked up several rocks and, using target practice as an excuse, zig-zagged through the woods.

A few times she seemed to catch sight of a shadow two or three hundred meters back. It was hard to tell; the trees were dense.

It was just as well they were – whoever was stalking her could not get a good shot at her either.

After fifteen minutes, Launa had had enough.

She found a spot on the river far enough away from the falls that it would not affect her hearing, and paused to wash her face and drink.

She heard rustling, then silence.

A moment later, the soft ratcheting of an arming handle told Launa all she needed to know. She considered how long it would take to draw a bead on a still target. Timing seemed about right.

She dropped.

Rapid automatic fire went over her head. She rolled into the river before the bad guy could correct his aim. She had picked this spot because the current ran fast and deep beside the rock.

Clutching her stones and sling, she dove deep, kicking for all she was worth as bullets sprayed the water.

———

J ack came awake to knocking. The sky was beginning to streak with pre-dawn colors outside his open window. He hit the light and raced for the door.

Opening it cautiously, he came face to face with Samantha. She held a long bowie knife that dripped blood.

She lunged for him.

He grabbed for her knife arm and was about to break it when she collapsed like a house of cards.

"Dick's dead," she said, her whisper hollow.

Jack pulled Samantha the rest of the way into his room. The flimsy gown she wore caught on the door. As he slammed it shut, most of what she was wearing got left in the hall.

Samantha was too far gone to notice.

"I woke up. Dick was beside me. This was sticking out of

him." She mumbled like a child. Her eyes focused on the knife, as if seeing it for the first time.

She dropped it. Blood smeared the beige carpet.

Jack picked it up. DM was carved on the pummel. No question who it belonged to. But who put it in its owner's back?

Jack turned for the phone, dragging Samantha with him. He lifted the receiver – silence.

He set Samantha on the bed, pulled out his bow and strung it. Slinging a quiver over his shoulder, he nocked an arrow, picked the administrator up, and half-carried her back into the hall.

She clung to him for security. Naked to reality, she sought shelter like a child.

Jack looked in both directions. The hallway was empty. He turned for Judith's room.

J udith pulled on her housecoat as she made her way to the door. She opened it to find Jack and Samantha standing there, one half-naked, and the other totally naked, looking for all the world like the lurid cover of a fantasy paperback.

"Captain Miller's dead," Jack snapped out. "The phones are too. You better get dressed. You got anything for her?"

Judith reached for Samantha just as Brent stuck his head out of his room. "What's happening?"

"The balloon's gone up. You better get some clothes on, old boy. Life's about to get interesting." Judith answered.

"Right-oh." Brent sounded too damn chipper for her money.

As Judith turned back to Samantha, Marilyn

cautiously edged out of her room. She was not wearing much either. Didn't anyone sleep in a decent nightie anymore?

However, the unwavering AR-15 was mostly what held Judith's attention.

Marilyn's eyes darted from person to person, taking in the scene before saying, "I'll be dressed in a second," and she was gone.

Jack unloaded Samantha on Judith, then edged into her doorway, blocking it to stand as hall monitor in his BVD's.

Judith led Samantha to her closet. She had two jump suits that would be best for whatever today held. Judith yanked one on, then helped Samantha into the other. She did not even try to zip it up all the way.

There was nothing sexy about the bureaucrat today. The real world had come calling, smashing her fantasy of control and power, leaving her as adrift as any orphaned waif.

Judith felt sorrow for her, but no sympathy.

By the time Judith rejoined Jack at the door, Brent was there, too. The old fellow carried a pistol, a relic of World War II.

Marilyn reappeared with a small arsenal. She and Brent stood guard to give Jack time to dress.

It took him only a minute, but he returned in full battle dress uniform. The sight of him in war dress, more than anything else this morning, told Judith matters had changed.

She shuddered as he borrowed Marilyn's pistol.

"I'll take point. Marilyn, will you cover the rear guard?"

She nodded.

"Brent, you stay with the women in the middle. Let's move slow and careful. There're friendlies out there with loaded weapons. They can kill you just as dead as the knife Samantha pulled out of Dick's back."

"Dick?" Marilyn echoed.

"He's dead," Samantha said, still made it sound like a question.

Marilyn scowled and turned to cover the rear, the muzzle of her rifle tracking the path of her eyes.

Jack led down the hall to the rear entrance. At the bottom of the stairs, Judith joined him. She searched the grounds as he did.

Nothing moved.

Jack signaled her to stay and began a hunched run toward the swimming pool.

"Halt." The voice was more menacing by its calm.

Jack froze. He held his gun away from him, but did not drop it. "We got a problem. Captain Miller's been killed and the phones are dead in the dormitories."

A ranch hand moved from behind a bush. The M-16 not leaving Jack as he spoke into a radio, then asked. "Who's with you, sir?"

"Judith, Samantha, Brent and Captain Brunner." Jack said, and signaled those behind him.

Judith stepped into the open, pulling Samantha. Brent waved his .45, then slipped back behind a brick wall, covering their questioner with his weapon.

Judith could not help wondering where men learned these silly games.

Two more cowboys appeared, weapons at the ready. In a minute, the Station Chief hustled up, hardly out of breath.

"Hell's a-popping everywhere. Teams have gone off net. Others have beat off suicide raids." His steel gray eyes searched the group. "Strange, we've only got one dead."

"Sir, Launa's out there. I've got to get her," Jack said.

The CIA man sucked on his lips. "I guess you do have to, son. Better draw body armor and a rifle. Take along a spare set for the girl, too," he added.

Jack was already off at a run.

Marilyn joined the group, setting the safety on her assault rifle. She went straight to Samantha's side. "You look like you could use some coffee."

The captain took the woman's arm and lead her toward the dining room.

Judith's ears were old, but she did not miss Marilyn's next words. "I know you've had a rough morning, but I'd like to talk again about the make-up of the teams."

Brent joined Judith as she watched the two women depart. He un-cocked his ancient automatic, then pointed it at the sky and pulled the trigger on an empty chamber. "I never trust these things."

"Guns don't kill people; people kill people," Judith quoted thoughtfully. "I'd like a cup of coffee, too."

Launa came up for air and dove quickly before the bullets caught her. Things got dicey as she careened through a series of small waterfalls. She did it well and if she lived, she would have the bruises and welts to prove it.

In the white water, she got a breath without coming under fire, but the calm pool below exploded with bullets when she came up for air.

The next series of falls included a turn in her favor. Her hunter would have to walk farther than she would have to swim. There was also a deadfall of trees at the bend. Massive trunks were knocked here and there like a child's game of sticks.

He would have to walk around that.

On the far side of the pool was a pebbled beach. Any sane person would be across it and running for the hills.

Launa was too mad to be sane.

Someone was trying to kill her and he was not too smart. The automatic weapon sounded like an AK-47. He had sprayed her like a street punk on a drive-by shooting – a stupid tactic for hitting a single target.

Launa wanted to meet this turkey. If she was unpredictable, she just might.

Bounding from the stream, she soaked the beach. She even left her sling and one moccasin scattered on the pebbles before she slipped back into the water.

Using an overhanging tree, she pulled herself up the rocky bank onto the other side and surveyed the situation.

The beach across from her looked like someone had made a panicked exit across it. The sling was no great loss; she was not about to trade rocks with automatic weapons fire.

No, she'd ambush her target and go hand to hand with the dumb punk.

She spotted a pathway down the rocky embankment that would probably be her hunter's avenue to the water.

A pole caught in the deadfall looked dangerous enough for her. An eroded space below the deadfall made for a good hiding place.

She had enough of running; it was time to kill something.

Concealed behind a rock overhang, Launa hunched down with her makeshift quarterstaff and made herself small. Listening, she ignored the noise of the waterfall.

She heard footsteps, one pair.

L auna's designated assassin fingered the trigger guard on his assault rifle, smiling as he glanced at the beach across from him. "Shit, have I got that broad on the run. I didn't need no three of us."

He would enjoy spending the extra money almost as much as he was enjoying chasing the army girl through the woods.

"She even left her little sling thing."

He flicked the safety on, then started down the rocky bank. A chunk slipped out from beneath his foot, he half fell to a large outcropping.

He was more careful as he looked for the rest of the way down to the water's edge. But even the fall did not spoil his fantasies. "I'm gonna have fun when I catch her. As long as I got a body to bring in, what do they care what I did with her?"

L auna cared very much what he did.

Murmuring a prayer of gratitude for the distraction of this guy's greed and lust, she listened to rocks slide, then footsteps as he found the expected path.

She readied herself for the lunge.

As she swung around the rock, he had his back to her, looking for the next step down.

She drove her pole into his neck, driving him forward, knocking him off balance. His head snapped back as he tumbled.

Pitching into the water, his forehead smashed against a rock on the way down.

Launa ran forward and snagged his gun sling with her pole. She wanted his weapon but she did not want a fight over it.

She weighed the advantages of capturing him, but the way his skull was dented, it seemed a moot question.

She reached for his gun; it would not come off. She held him under with the pole and studied the situation.

Bubbles escaped his mouth; he did not struggle.

A sick feeling grew in Launa's gut. She was looking at death for the first time. Death was part of her profession. She knew it, but she had never faced it like this.

Launa felt bile rise in her empty stomach. Tightening every muscle, she willed herself to stay in control.

Carefully, she rolled him over. He slipped off the rock and sank; gun, ammunition, boots, and all.

"Damn. I want that gear." She used her pole to search for him.

Two minutes later the body went over the small falls at the end of the pool. Moments later, a sodden mass hung for a moment at the next fall then plunged over.

It was a big cascade. She hiked around to it.

Halfway down the fall, wedged between rocks, was the guy who wanted her dead.

The tumbling water smashed his head against the rock again and again. The face was gone. The skull was shattered. Brains and blood colored the foam.

"Well, Jack, I hope now you'll give me credit for taking care of myself," she shouted.

Then she was sick.

10

L auna headed downstream as fast as she dared. When she heard a helicopter coming, she dodged into the woods. She had enough surprises.

The chopper came in low and fast. As the Huey passed her, she spotted Jack in the co-pilot's seat.

Breaking cover, she stumbled over a rock. The chopper was gone before she recovered.

Five minutes later, she heard rotor blades again and waited near a bush. It looked like the same one, so she did not hide.

It passed her, looped around and hovered over the stream in front of her. Jack stepped out on the runners carrying several things, then dropped into the water.

Despite his three-week growth of beard, Jack was in BDU's, battle dress uniform.

A cold chill swept over Launa. He had not been in uniform since the day she volunteered.

Jack's load came into focus as he waded toward her carrying M-16s and body armor. Maybe she wasn't the only one with problems this morning.

The helicopter lifted and flew over the trees behind her. She kept her eyes on Jack. As he reached the bank, he looked her full in the face.

"Someone blew up the Leader's chancellery last night, but missed him. I'm sorry for the dumbest, most pig-headed, shit-for-brains stunt I've ever pulled in my life, but while you were safe out here, someone killed Miller and several other teams were suicide bombed. In the rush this morning, I didn't get your clothes, but here's body armor and a rifle."

Launa reached for the M-16. "You sure you trust me with a gun?" she asked, loading a bullet into the chamber. weapon.

"With my life." The words were simple. Even in her anger, Launa could taste the absolute.

"Good, because you'll find a body dangling from a water fall two miles back. He had an AK-47. We've all had our troubles this morning, Captain."

Launa made the rank a slap.

Jack shot a worried glance upstream, then faced her. "Yes, ma'am. If you'll come with me."

He wrapped the body armor around her.

She put her arms through the holes. *So, this is what the well un-dressed centerfold is wearing this week.*

Like most armor she had tried on, it was too big for her. She might not get arrested for indecent exposure. If anyone complained, she'd shoot 'em before she'd take any more crap. She'd faced an assault gun today and killed a man bare handed. She was ready for any army.

Deferentially, Jack kicked stones out of her path. She let him. He owed her a lot. The helicopter waited in a clearing.

It lifted as she was belting in and quickly gained speed.

Launa watched the forest race past, fondling her rifle,

struggling with feelings. She had survived. She had killed. She was ready now. God help anyone who got in her way.

She looked at Jack's helmeted head. The boy had better behave.

Judith looked up from the pad she had been making notes on when the female comm tech raced up to the table Marilyn and Samantha were sitting at.

"The chopper just radioed in – they've got Launa. Somebody tried to slab her, but she wasted the guy. Bare-assed with just a pole, she blew away an asshole with an AK-47. Now that's my kind of woman."

The tech grinned at everyone, then, without so much as a nod to Samantha, strode away.

Brent's eyes followed the tech. "That's one happy woman. Maybe a bit jealous, but happy."

Judith had kept her eyes on the other table. Marilyn had not taken the good news well at all. In a second, she was up and following the tech out.

"That is not a happy woman. How far does her jealousy go?" Judith mused through a frown.

Brent shook his head slowly.

A still-shaken Samantha fumbled her way to their table. "I think I've made a terrible mistake. Marilyn tried to get me to send her and Jack as a team. I don't think she expected Launa back."

The woman swayed, holding on to a chair for support. Then all color left her face. "Dick and I were leaving Harvey's Place last night when we spotted Marilyn using a phone. She must have seen us. She hung up and started yelling at us to get back here. Why didn't I say something about this earlier?"

Her long fingernails dug into the white flesh of her palms, drawing blood.

Judith stood, taking Samantha's hands in her own. "Too much has happened too fast, but I think we better go see the station chief."

Judith was surprised that Samantha and Brent kept up the pace she set.

They were ten minutes out from the ranch when Jack unbuckled and came to sit beside Launa. He doffed his helmet and handed it to her as he leaned close to shout.

"Marilyn disappeared after they announced you were coming back. The station chief suggests the pilot drop us off and make the approach to the ranch without us. He's game."

The pilot glanced back at Launa, grinned and gave her a thumbs-up. He looked too young to have flown in Nam or even Saudi.

"He won't have any gun support," Launa shouted back.

"They'll have rifles scattered around the ranch."

"You and I could do it better."

"If we get killed, who takes the mission?" Jack's eyes never left hers.

"They've got other teams."

Jack shook his head.

"That bad?"

He nodded.

"Does she have any ground to air rockets?" Launa called to the pilot.

He spoke into the radio. Almost a minute passed. Then

he shook his head. "None missing from supply or checked out to that team. But she's got a shit pot of explosives. They've found a couple already and defused them."

Launa wanted Marilyn. She knew it was personal, but the blood lust was up. "Let's force her hand. We go in fast and high."

Launa flipped the safety off her weapon. "Which side do you want?"

Jack went to the right-hand door and buckled himself in. Launa went to the left, arranged the armor to do the most good, and cinched herself in.

The wind felt good on her bare skin. Suddenly she understood the crazy Vikings who stripped and charged the enemy completely naked but for an ax. Maybe there was something to them after all.

The ranch came in sight. They were high. The pilot had just started a powered descent when he shouted. "Hot LZ! Two o`clock."

"Damn!" Launa cursed as Jack squeezed off a three-round burst, then another, and another. The chopper filled with the acrid smell of his gunfire.

Angry bees smashed through the cabin. The plexiglass windscreen shattered in a howling gale. The whine of the turbine changed. The rate of descent picked up.

The Huey lurched to the right, began to spin. Launa saw smoke out her window. A building exploded in what must have been the two o'clock position.

The chopper slowed its dive, then smashed into the ground.

In a moment, Jack was standing over her, releasing her seat belt, helping her. She half-stumbled and was half-carried from the wreckage.

Two men ran to the pilot. He was slumped in his

harness, a large splotch of dark spreading over the chest of his green flight suit.

Launa's legs turned to jelly and the ground came up quickly.

Jack scooped her up as she fell.

Judith was beside them. "The poor girl's totally spent. Can you carry her to her room?"

"Yes."

Launa wanted to say something, but used the last strength she had to keep her jaws set against the emptiness her gut struggled to vomit out.

She let the darkness come.

L auna came awake to a knocking at her door. The clock told her she had slept two hours.

"Come in." Her voice was weak, but Jack entered. Launa lay under two blankets. Groggy, she pulled herself up. Looking at him, she fingered the neck of the nightshirt she now wore.

"Judith evicted me and put you to bed. She's still rather old fashioned. You should have seen the flannel nightgown she was wearing this morning."

But Launa's eyes were for what he carried. He put down his rifle and held up the uniform he had slung over his arm. "Your first set of BDU's, complete with butter bars."

Actually, the rank insignias were camouflage black, not the gold of a second lieutenant, but Launa's grin knew no limit.

"Your presence is requested at a working lunch. Can you make it?"

"If I can get to the shower, I just might live."

Launa slowly rolled out of bed, groaning only twice. Jack hung the uniform in the bathroom and started water running. Launa rummaged in her dresser for the necessary underwear, then shoved him out of the bathroom and closed the door.

She had no strength so she showered quickly. When she presented herself in the open doorway, Jack was hovering beside it, as if he thought she might need a lifeguard. He had searched her closet and had her boots ready.

"You look good, Lieutenant."

"Thank you." She felt a lot better.

"Can I help you on with your boots?"

For a moment, hard independence flashed in her gut, then she let it out with a sigh. "I need to sit down. I'd appreciate the help."

She plopped into the room's single stuffed chair and stared into space while he put on her socks and laced up her boots. The touch of his hands on her feet returned sensuality to a heart she thought was eternal stone.

He offered her a hand up when he was done. She took it gratefully. "I think I was crazy there for a while."

He retrieved his M-16. As he locked the door to her room, he spoke. "You hadn't had much to eat. Your body was burning a lot to keep going. Since this morning, you must have been going on adrenalin alone. That would make anybody crazy. And spent," he added.

"I'd hate to become crazy like Marilyn."

Jack nodded and followed Launa's slow pace down the stairs to the dining room.

A long table was set with cold cuts. The drapes were pulled closed and the windows covered with masking tape. All except one. Covered with plywood, it was a casualty of the morning.

Judith and Brent, the CIA chief, and Samantha, joined them. Enough weapons to topple most governments were carefully placed on tables within easy reach.

Launa started heaping meat on a sandwich. When Jack added beans and potato salad to her plate, she gave him a grateful smile.

"What's happening in the world?" Judith asked.

"Negotiations didn't go too well." The CIA man's words were dry as kindling. "They met the head of the Movement. He wants to be called 'The Leader'."

"That's Fuhrer in German." Brent noted.

"Yeah." The old timer nodded. Launa stopped a fork full of beans half way to her mouth, trying to recall all she could about the leader of the Third Reich.

"The new Fuhrer didn't beat around the bush. For the next twenty years he wants three trillion dollars a year from the developed world. Calls it 'tribute'. If he doesn't get it, he'll attack Europe."

"This guy doesn't sound very reasonable." Jack frowned.

Brent shook his head "That's one of the risks you take. With a reasonable person, offers and counter-offers lead to solutions. Power-oriented people mistake offers for concessions. A willingness to talk is mistaken for weakness which they seek to dominate."

"What are we going to do?" Launa asked, looking from face to face.

"Not much we can do," the CIA man said with a shrug. "Somebody sold the Libyans the new French radars that can spot stealth aircraft. They're deployed around the Chinese-made missiles that satellite imagery shows are locked and loaded in Uganda. Our Generals don't think the missiles will fly anywhere near the two Russian anti-missile sites.

"Since the Europeans don't have a missile defense

system, we're flying to Europe anything that has a chance of shooting one down. The President and his people are putting together a new offer – one with more money that is coated with threats and demands."

"Frightening, isn't it?" Judith said, shaking her head ruefully. "Now they cooperate – but with no idea how to confront a dominator. It happens again."

Launa finished off the last bit of sandwich and reached for more fixings. "That covers the world. How are things here? Is the chopper pilot alright?"

The CIA chief shook his head. "We've got four dead, including him, Dick, and Marilyn. A number of wounded, none bad. Marilyn blew up most of your pottery and fiber, but the copper and bronze gear survived. So did the animals. With minor exceptions, you are mission capable. That's more than I can say for the other teams."

"How bad are they?" Samantha asked. To Launa's surprise, she sounded concerned.

"Pretty bad. I don't think any team has enough personnel to send a full complement. We're it."

"And Livermore?" Launa said with a worried frown.

"They got hit, but they beat it off with no problem. The bad guys showed up at the wrong gate."

"That's probably the way Marilyn arranged it." Samantha's voice sounded weak and distant. "I'll bet she was manipulating the Movement while they thought they were controlling her. She sure did want to go. With everyone else dead, she and Jack would be the only ones left to send."

"I wonder how long I'd have lived?" Jack said, glancing Launa's way.

"She wanted to be empress of the world," Judith said. "She saw a chance to make it happen. When everything started slipping away, I guess she threw in with the Leader."

Marilyn was crazy, Launa reflected, but how sane was she today?

Samantha shivered. "I'm glad we caught her before the jump. Think of the trouble she would have made once she was there. She wouldn't have cared one whit about history."

"That's how most history is made," Judith snapped. "By people who can't see past what they want today. I hope this lesson isn't lost on all present." Her face was hard as she searched first Jack's, then Launa's eyes.

Neither flinched.

Samantha brought them back to the present. "We're awaiting orders. While the Secretary of State flies back to Washington, nothing's happening. We need to get you two in for shots and final medical. As soon as they can break an airplane loose, you'll probably be ordered to Livermore."

"Brent and I are making some last preparations also," Judith said.

The station chief pushed back from the table. "My people will try to clean up this mess and make sure you're not disturbed again. Everybody got weapons?"

All nodded, except Judith. She shook her head firmly.

"May I persuade you to at least carry a cane?"

Judith frowned. The CIA Chief offered her an ornate walking cane, then detached the head to show a wicked blade.

She took it.

"You look very distinguished," Brent guffawed, "for an old lady."

Judith hit him with the cane.

The day was full. There were not enough seconds in each minute.

Gear had to be checked for damage. Jack insisted they work out, "To relieve tension and help with all those shots."

He kept it gentle and Launa was grateful.

Over supper, Judith admitted that she and Brent had a few more phone calls to make before they were ready to pick a time and place.

As evening came on, Launa was still sore from the shots. A jacuzzi session did not help. She paused at her door.

"I'm too keyed up to sleep."

"Me too. Think a walk would help?"

They hefted their rifles and headed out the back way. A guard materialized at their elbow before they got to the archery range. "Where y'all headed, sir?"

"A walk, maybe a chance to talk. Day's been kind of busy," Jack said.

"Has been kind of like that. Any particular direction?"

"Out to the rim of the cap-rock," Launa said.

The man turned away and spoke into his headset, then turned back. "Y'all walk slow and don't try sneaking around anything. We're kind of nervous tonight."

"Maybe we ought to forget this." Launa said.

"I'd really like to have a chance to talk." Jack didn't keep a pleading undertone out of his voice. Launa relented.

The guard reached in his pocket. "Here's a Chemlite. Tonight's color is blue. Use it when you come back into the perimeter."

They walked in silence. Jack had slung his rifle. His hands were stuffed deep in his pockets. Launa fiddled with the light.

"Was this your first time to face a gun?" Jack didn't look at her as he spoke.

"There was something in high school, but I didn't think he'd use the gun on me." Launa had not thought much of it then. Compared to today, it was nothing.

She shivered as she again saw bubbles breaking the surface, a face bashed to mush on the rocks, a pilot slumped over his collective who had still gotten his passengers down.

"What about you, Jack?" Launa asked, turning her mind away from her own demons.

"You know about Saudi. I saw enough action with the 24th Mech even if it didn't turn out to be much of a fight. I never thought the aftermath of a war 'won' would be harder to face than the war, but it was." Jack got silent again. Launa let the quiet hang although she wanted to scream at him to say whatever was on his mind.

They were half way to the rim before Jack turned to her. "Launa, I'm sorry about that stupid hike. The only excuse I can give you is I needed to know you could take care of yourself. I care about you – maybe too much. You're a very good soldier, Launa, a good comrade, but you're more than that to me."

That was not what Launa wanted to hear. "God damn it, Jack. I am not Sandy and I'm never going to take her place. Just because the Army has thrown us together and I look like her does not mean that you need to protect me like your wife!"

"Whoa. Time out, woman." Jack took two steps back, held his hands up in a crossed "T."

"What the hell are you talking about? Nobody could fill Sandy's place. I've spent three years learning that lesson and I've got it down solid. And who said you looked like her? If anybody around here looked the part, it's Samantha, for Christ's sake. As for protection, Sandy was one woman who could take very good care of herself and wouldn't let anyone forget that. Launa, what gave you any idea. . ." Jack stopped, puzzled

Now it was Launa's turn to stumble back. For a moment, the silence of the night held them. "Marilyn told me I looked like Sandy."

"Marilyn never met Sandy."

"But she told me . . . I think I've been had, Captain."

"I think we've both been had by one manipulative bitch. Every time we met she always managed to mention your inexperience and somehow dig at how you'd handle yourself if I died." Jack shook his head.

"I took survival training in Panama and Bahrain."

"It wasn't in your file."

"I know. I was an Army brat then and I've been too mad to tell you these past weeks."

"I'm sorry."

"I guess I haven't been handling myself too well. You were right; we shouldn't have ridden that chopper in this morning and if that asshole back in the hills had had any smarts about him, he would have gotten me."

Launa gulped, a tremor went through her as she realized how close she had come to death twice today.

"You did better than any other soldier I know, man or woman."

All her life, Launa had wanted to hear such praise from the colonel. She never had. Then Jack opened his arms and suddenly that was the only place she wanted to be.

It was not much of a hug; they were both toting an armory, and metal got in the way. But for Launa, there was more comfort in Jack's arms than any place she could recall in her twenty-one years. It went on for a long time. While he held her, the images of death stayed at bay.

Jack had been talking for some time before Launa realized it. "When I lost Sandy and Sam, I swore I'd never get close to another human being. It hurt too much and I didn't want to hurt like that again. I didn't think another woman could ever mean anything to me. These last three weeks, working with you, I found one very special person, like no one else I've ever met. In spite of myself, I think I'm falling in love with you."

Launa started at the word, but before she could react, there was noise behind them. They both brought M-16's off their shoulders in one fluid motion, safeties clicking off. A blue light showed about a hundred meters off. "Captain, Lieutenant. We got more message traffic coming in. Skipper said you'd want to hear it."

Launa flipped the safety back on. Jack was slower. "Show yourself."

The guard's camouflage was good. Even with the light, they could hardly see him. Mainly it was his motion against the starlit backdrop that Launa's eyes traced. He walked in, his gun held out to his left.

"How'd you know where to find us?" Jack's voice started to relax.

"We got pick-up mikes scattered around."

Launa wondered how much of their heart-felt talk was now on tape. It did not seem to matter. That she had not answered Jack mattered much to her.

The comm center was alive with everyone by the time they returned. The Station Chief took center stage. "The Leader just delivered an ultimatum."

He scanned down his message sheet. "The usual crap. The price is still three trillion. He wants an agreement by noon day-after-tomorrow or he will retaliate."

"Retaliate?" Brent looked half-asleep, but the word caught his attention.

"Retaliate. He seems to think we're already at war."

"Somebody ought to teach that boy something about logic," the old scholar grumbled.

Launa saw a bigger problem. "Does that ultimatum expire at noon Nairobi time, European, or Washington?"

The CIA chief shook his head. "I don't know. Good question."

A com tech handed the Chief a message. He grinned like a cougar smelling prey. "Listen up folks, we got orders at last. A C-5 will be here at 0800 local time to pick up the team. They want you folks at Livermore early tomorrow."

"All right!"

"About time!"

"Thought they'd forgotten us."

The room bubbled with enthusiasm. Launa turned to Jack. He nodded gravely. They had orders, the orders they had hoped never to get.

11

———

The wake-up call was scheduled for 0500. Launa came awake from a nightmare she could not remember. As she picked up the phone, the clock beside it said 0730. "What the hell?"

"Things are moving kind of slow this morning," a voice drawled. "Judith and Samantha thought you could use some extra sleep. The Chief agreed."

"Where's Jack?"

"I just called him, Ma'am. He asked for you to meet him in five minutes."

She hung up and reached for her gear.

The work out was good, but her body had been wasted by the last few days. Again, Jack kept things gentle and words few.

Over a late breakfast, Judith brought them up to date on what was happening. "The Secretary of State is back, but the President has delayed the Tele-Summit until sometime later today. Time's still not set."

Launa winced as she reached for an apple. "That's

cutting it close. Does anyone know when the ultimatum expires?"

Judith shook her head. "I think the President is hoping to stretch it to the limit by not getting it cleared up."

Jack frowned. "That may not be too smart."

Judith just shrugged.

Launa bit into her apple. "Why'd we get to sleep in?" She hated to squander time.

"Someone sent our C-5 to Frankfort. The replacement they assigned us blew an engine on take-off from Dover. They finally snatched one at Tinker that was scheduled for an overhaul, but they hadn't started on it yet. They're trying to shanghai a crew now. The Chief doesn't want to leave here until the plane's ninety minutes out."

Launa shook her head. Hell was knocking and it was business as usual. "Let's just hope this bird will stay in the air."

The morning went slowly. Several off-duty guards started a baseball game. Jack and Launa exercised the horses and dogs. Afterwards, he showed her what he had collected.

"If we can get it there, I prefer not to take it." Still, four bows, six quivers of flint-tipped arrows and two quarter staffs with large flint spear points were at the top of his list. Several copper axe heads, digging mattocks, and copper-edged scythes were laid out and packed away in leather bags. Copper and bronze tools, trading goods of shells, red ocher, and obsidian, were also put carefully away.

A separate bag held rough chunks of raw copper and tin. "Most of the clay cooking vessels and bowls were smashed yesterday. I prefer to take metal anyway."

Weavers had provided warm, brightly colored blankets and baskets to hold gear. Jack had fashioned pack frames to hang the baskets on the horses. "Much of this we'll cache and go back for. I just don't want to arrive penniless."

"I notice a lot of copper, but not much bronze."

"Still no word whether we're going to the Bronze Age or before." Jack said with a fatalistic shrug.

Word finally came over lunch that their plane was in the air. They finished eating.

As Judith helped Launa finish packing, Maria approached with a finely tooled leather bag.

"This is the book my daughter gave me on herbal medicine. I'm sorry I didn't get it to you sooner." She offered it to Launa. "Take it with you. You can study it on the plane. It will help you."

"But I'm not sure I'll be able to get it back to you."

"That is okay. You will need it. Take it."

Accepting the leather bag, Launa felt the weight of the book inside. She clasped it to her breast tightly; it felt warm, like the sun.

Launa knew how to fight and kill; this book could teach her how to heal and take away suffering. Would there be time to memorize all it offered her?

Maria drew Launa into a hug. "Go with God," she whispered then turned back toward the kitchen.

Launa watched her go. As a soldier, Launa was sworn to protect women like Maria. It did not look like many people in power were giving the likes of this woman much thought. What could a lone lieutenant do for all the Marias of the world?

Launa did not know, but with a set to her jaw, she swore she would find out.

The Station Chief got his convoy underway right on time. Launa had not expected it, but sympathy welled up in her as she watched Samantha standing alone on the veranda as they drove out. She was being left behind by developments.

The dominator had become another victim, another nothing.

The C-5 was on its latest revised schedule. It landed as they drove up to Jackson Hole Municipal Airport.

Twenty minutes later, the horse trailer was tied down and airmen were hard at work loading the second trailer full of mission-critical gear. The load master moved with speed and purpose.

Launa and Jack stayed with the dogs and horses for the take-off. Once things settled down, the horse wrangler offered to take over. They climbed the stairs to the upper deck where Brent and Judith had taken the two most forward seats.

Launa rummaged in the luggage, found her duffle, and extracted Maria's leather bag. She followed Jack down the aisle to one of the rear seats. Seated next to him, she opened the book and began to study it. Maria had said there was an herb that was as good as aspirin for pain. Launa searched for it.

She found Jack looking over her shoulder. "I remember that weed. It grew in the hills behind our house, before they built condos up there. Dad had the gardeners destroy any that took root on our lawn."

"This says it's good for stomach cramps and ulcers," she said.

For the next several minutes she and Jack read, starting from the first page, then Jack reached over, used a finger to mark their place, and closed the book.

"Last night, you and I started to talk," his words hardly carried above the cabin noise. Launa looked down at where his hands had covered hers and swallowed.

Her feelings were so mixed up today, toward Jack the man, Jack the soldier ,and the crazy world that summoned them to God-only-knew-what. Did she want to talk about love?

"I made a fool of myself," Jack continued. "Sending you into the back country was one of the stupidest moves ever made in military history."

Launa remembered to breathe. Jack was not proposing to talk about love. She sloughed off her anxiety like an over-weight pack – and remembered she was supposed to be mad at him.

"Three weeks ago, I promised you and Judith I'd take a leaf out of the Old Neolith's book on leadership and be your partner. I screwed that up pretty bad. I'm not going to have a chance to get it better with more prac-tice, so I made up my mind while you were out there to quit."

"Quit!" Launa gasped. Who was there to go with? What was he doing on this plane?

"Quit being the senior partner in this exercise." Jack rushed on. "From now on, you're in charge. You take the lead and I follow. If we get there and women are in charge, you've got it. You tell me and I do it – no questions asked, no back-talk. Until then, I practice." He looked into her eyes, unblinking.

Launa frowned back at him. He did not do things in half measures; three days from running her around the boonies like some plebe to making her the general. Shit. That was not what she wanted.

What she really wanted was his hide nailed to the barn door.

She blinked and broke away from his gaze. She and he were on an airplane flying them to duty. What they might personally want was not part of the mission profile. She turned to Jack, her eyes as icy as her heart.

"Captain, I was counting on you to teach me what I needed to learn. I was counting on you cover where I was weak. Instead, you sent me off to learn what I didn't need to know and now you're turning the lead over to me before I'm properly prepared because you screwed it."

Jack nodded without any hint of a flinch.

Damn he's good when he's good.

"I will be senior partner wherever they chose to send us, but you better sure as hell give me your opinion when I need it and your obedience when I ask for it."

"You have it, Launa."

"Then let's get back to studying."

She was amazed at how fast the flight passed with the two of them reading.

A Blackhawk waited, rotors turning, as the C-5 taxied to a stop at Moffett. The four moved quickly to it. Others would take care of their luggage and equipment.

The flight to Livermore was short. As the chopper circled to land, Launa stared out the window. The west gate now was a blackened hole, twenty meters across. A visitors' center and trees were flattened.

Brent and Judith hustled off as soon as the chopper settled on the helipad. Two people in white lab coats came to greet Jack and Launa.

"Someone new doing your landscaping?" Jack quipped to a short man who shook his head.

"We've got the transporter forty feet underground where it couldn't be damaged."

"Transporter, as in 'Beam me up, Scotty'?" Launa's esti-
mation of the science team went up a notch. At least
someone had a sense of humor.

Jack introduced Dr. Milo, the pudgy head of the team
who smiled as he took Launa's hand. "We couldn't think of
anything else to call it.

Beside him stood Dr. Harrison, a tall woman, who wore
her brown hair in a tight bun. It was she who first noticed
the temporal displacement. She shook Launa's hand firmly.
"Hungry?"

"We missed supper," Launa said as she shook her hand.
"I could eat a horse."

The cafeteria was a short walk away. The two doctors
took only coffee. Even while Jack joined Launa in loading a
tray, he got down to business with a question.

"I brought three horses. What's the weight limit?"

This was the first Launa had heard of a weight limit. She
swore under her breath, wondering what else she was
missing from her briefings.

Harrison elbowed her beaming supervisor. "The boss
here doesn't believe in sleep. We've extended the machine's
capacity significantly this last week."

"We'll have the test results early tomorrow. You'll be
quite happy." Dr. Milo clearly was.

At this hour, the dining room was nearly empty. Launa
chose a table by the window. As she got down to serious
eating, she asked a double barreled question of the two
doctors.

"What went wrong with the first test? Will this thing
work now?"

The two doctors exchanged worried looks, which did
not help Launa's digestion.

Dr. Milo put down his coffee before saying, "I believe it

worked the first time. It's my fault we do not know for sure." He slumped in his chair.

"Merv is too hard on himself." Dr. Harrison put a hand on his arm. "The isotopes we sent were a good way to calibrate our equipment. We dated our package to within minutes of its arrival."

Launa gulped to empty her mouth and paused with a spoonful of carrots in her hand. "Is that important?"

"Very." Dr. Harrison's head bobbed for emphasis. "I'll explain in a minute, but let me finish with Muffin."

"Muffin?" Launa got the word out as she stuffed carrots in.

Both Doctors smiled. "Muffin," Dr. Milo repeated, "was a cute mutt we picked up at the pound. We wanted to test our system with live tissue. The question was how to verify the successful transportation of a living creature. We had all sorts of wild ideas. One was to plant a bomb on Muffin that would explode when she was fifty feet away from the landing point."

"That was terrible." Dr. Harrison broke in.

Dr. Milo shook his head. "If we'd done it, we'd know what happened. I'm a physicist," he scowled out the window. "A soft-hearted, maybe soft in the head physicist. Biologists sacrifice animals all the time. I never had. I thought we could send Muffin and the isotopes back. If we found the isotopes, we would know Muffin had arrived and when. If we found Muffin's collar and bones with the isotopes, we'd know the trip was lethal. If Muffin survived, she would take off and live a happy life among the Indians and we would find nothing."

"That's what happened, isn't it?" Launa interrupted buttering a piece of sourdough bread to study the two doctors.

"Probably." Harrison agreed. Carefully she sloshed coffee in her cup. After a long pause, she continued. "But the shock wave confuses the issue. We may have scattered Muffin's bones over the last thousand years. We've searched the hill and offered a reward for the collar. So far, nothing."

Launa put her bread down, no longer hungry. "I was afraid of something like that."

Dr. Harrison shook her head. "No, no. It is very likely the heavy isotopes' radiation caused the shock wave. I would bet my life that the transporter will work."

Dr. Milo crumpled his empty paper coffee cup. "My dear Betty, these people are doing just that." He let that thought hang in the air for several moments before he glanced at his watch. "We'd better get to the bunker."

Launa set a slow pace as they left the cafeteria. For the first time, she fully understood the risks involved.

It was frightening enough that the world was at risk and her attempt to change that might mean leaving behind everything she had ever known. Yet the possibility that she could be killed for even attempting that mission, clogged her throat with frustration.

She breathed deep of the warm California air, swallowing the emotions that threatened her. She let her eyes wander the blue sky and brown hills. A line of windmills marched across the eastern ridge. Only half were working.

"What are those?" Buried deep in her feelings another question nagged at Launa, but she could not find it. Better the inane.

"Oh, something left over from the seventies," Dr. Harrison said with a shrug. "There was a tax break then, so a lot of windmills were built. The break ran out and oil was cheap. As long as they run, it's fine. When one stops, that's it. Time ran out on them."

Launa remembered her question. "Why did you need to know the exact arrival time of the test run?"

"Time travel involves temporal displacement and movement through space." Doctor Milo gestured as he talked. "The earth is not where it was yesterday. Even if you were to go back a year, the sun has moved. We've computed exactly when and where to put you."

"So you'll send us to the Danube river basin from here."

"Right." Harrison added. "One ticket gets you both places. Think of the money we're saving."

"And if you send us into the middle of a mountain?" Launa raised the traditional science fiction problem.

"There will be a big boom," the short physicist said, then shrugged.

They went inside. A bank of elevators offered to take them up or down. Dr. Harrison pushed for the lowest floor. Two armed guards greeted them, ran their ID cards through a computer check, then scratched their names off a short list.

The conference room they entered was large, yet the heavy wooden table in the middle made it look small. One wall held large flat monitors and all the chairs faced it. Three screens showed similar conference rooms under the headings of The Hague, Moscow, and Washington. The screens were blank.

Brent hailed Launa. The four of them went to meet Brent, who, with Judith, was surrounded by a half-dozen people in business dress. Judith inundated Launa with a round of introductions that left her none the wiser, except now she had officially met the Rand part of the project.

"While you were with Dr. Milo, the Secretary of State briefed the people on net."

"You got a presidential briefing!" Launa snapped. "What did we miss?"

"Not a thing." Brent said through tight lips.

"Our mikes weren't live." Judith explained. "I don't think the Europeans or Russians knew we were on net. The President will want to talk to us in a few minutes."

"What's happening?" Launa insisted, angry at being left out.

"Nothing you didn't already know. President Lark wants to deliver a counter ultimatum an hour before theirs is due to expire. We'll offer more aid and demand they dismantle their rockets."

Whatever else Judith might have said was cut off as the cameras and mikes came on. They were broadcasting live to the White House.

Jack and Launa stood at rigid attention.

"You people out there hear us?" The Commander in Chief asked.

"Yes, Sir." Launa and Jack answered in unison before the civilians could react. Admiral Benson, Chairman of the Joint Chiefs, grinned as if his own kids had done him proud.

"There's not much they can do besides get a good night's sleep, is there Admiral?" the president said amicably. "The ultimatum will expire at seven o'clock tomorrow morning and we won't need to involve them until then."

"Yes, Mr. President. 1200 Zulu is 0400 hours in California." The Admiral corrected the President without actually doing so.

"Well, I wanted you to know what we're up against and what we're doing. Get some sleep. I will be."

The President grinned confidently as the screen went blank.

Launa frowned at Jack, wondering what had just happened.

"Launa, you and I should get some sack time and leave a wakeup call for 0300."

"I thought the President wanted our advice," Brent said, then snorted.

"When men of power want your opinion, they'll give it to you," Judith said with a smile, but the bitterness behind it was lost on no one.

When Judith and Brent turned to join some associates, Launa and Jack left.

12

The shower helped Launa shake the vague memory of nightmares she felt but did not recall. Putting on her dress greens for the first time, she ignored her shaggy hair in the mirror and admired the gold bars glittering on her shoulders.

As they downed a quick breakfast of pancakes and scrambled eggs in the cafeteria, Jack looked a bit strange in his dress greens and beard.

They were in the bunker conference room at 0345. It was empty.

Then the monitors suddenly lit up.

Jack drifted toward the screens for a better look. The Hague showed people running around, waving papers. Others milled in small groups.

Jack pulled on his beard. "Looks like a Chinese fire drill to me."

The Moscow screen lit up with a bit more sedate picture.

"What's going on? How do we get sound?" Launa searched the room for controls, then gave up. She dared not touch anything.

"I think something happened. Where the hell's Washington?"

As if to answer him, the White House came on-line. So did their sound. Launa recognized President Schmerling of the European Confederation.

"President Lark," the European cried, "the Movement launched its attack before the ultimatum expired, immediately upon getting your counter proposal."

Jack and Launa both inhaled sharply.

The American President blanched and stammered. "Did they . . . Did the missiles . . . I mean, was anything hit?"

"We're trying to find out. This place is a mad house. No one knows anything." The sharp edge to the European President's voice added to the tension. "Won't somebody tell me something?"

The U.S. President turned to Admiral Benson. "What have we got?"

The admiral was in the left-hand corner of the screen, almost off camera. He raised a hand, waving the Commander-in-Chief to silence.

President Lark's face began to redden.

Half a minute later, the Chairman turned and made his way quickly to his irritated Chief Executive.

"Mr. President, if you'll step aside, I'll brief you."

"These are our allies. For God's sake, what's happened?"

The admiral frowned, adjusted his coat, and began speaking to the cameras. "Space Command analyzed the satellite pickups and E-3 uplinks. All eighteen missiles initiated launch between 1116 and 1118 Zulu. Three missiles self-destructed in the first minute of flight."

Admiral Benson glanced down at a fax. "It appears the payloads ruptured on those three. We must assume biological agents are spreading downwind from them."

The admiral turned to the President. "Sir, all fifteen of the remaining missiles blew up on reentry over Europe, between 40,000 and 100,000 feet. We didn't fire a single shot."

"Huh." The President's mouth dropped open.

"I would guess the flasks for the biological agents were not stressed properly. When the vehicle heated up on reentry, they exploded. My little granddaughter could explain what happened." said the admiral with a dry chuckle.

Bedlam broke out. One would think the three command groups had won the World Soccer Cup. But then they had.

The U.S. President pounded his National Security Advisor on the shoulders. One cabinet level official threw a cup of coffee in the air. Everywhere people laughed and slapped each other on the back.

In the background, the admiral gazed at a world map, stroking his chin, a worried frown deepening the lines on his face.

Shivers went down Launa's spine.

Jack's eyes swiveled between her and the Admiral and back. He set his jaw. "We got problems," he whispered softly.

"What do you think they are?" Launa asked, though she strongly suspected she knew.

"You said it three weeks ago on the flight out, Lieutenant. Somebody's let the genie out of the bottle. It's not back in yet."

Gradually, the admiral's worried demeanor sobered the groups.

Finally, President Lark turned to him. "Chuck, you look like a man who threw a party and forgot to come."

"Mr. President, I'm not sure." His arms dropped to his side, half at attention as he turned. "I'd like to assume the explosions destroyed the virus. With your permission, I'll have some U-2's and TR-1's make air sampling runs. They can get to 80,000 feet plus."

He turned to the Soviet President. "Your country is downwind. May we overfly you?"

President Drozdov frowned. "Is this necessary?"

"Maybe it isn't. We won't know until we check."

The Soviet consulted with his advisers. Finally, Drozdov turned back to the Admiral. "We have need of your aircraft. However, some republics will frown upon this extension of our 'Open Skies' agreement if they feel it is used to our disadvantage." He left the statement at that.

Benson nodded to the Soviet. "Mr. President, I suspect some of my Air Force colleagues will hemorrhage, however, I invite you to send observers to our Metro Tango base in western Germany to observe that the TR-1's assigned to overfly your country have their cameras removed. God knows, maybe that'll help them get higher. With our European friends' permission, we will go ahead with this."

It took a moment for anyone in The Hague to react. The speed at which their situation kept changing was taking its toll.

Prime Minister Fleury finally nodded. "Yes, but of course."

"I have to get the mission started. If you'll excuse me." Admiral Benson nodded to the president and left.

The President slumped in his chair like a rag doll. Washington was silent, frozen in time.

President Drozdov finally stood up. "If we have no further information, I suggest we adjourn, but keep this line open. May I also suggest we have our health officials in attendance when next we meet?"

The other Presidents nodded numbly. Moscow's screen went gray, then The Hague, then Washington.

Livermore was forgotten.

Jack turned to Launa. "I think we're in trouble."

All the nightmares Launa could not remember crowded around her. All the terrors she had kept at arm's length for the last month danced at her elbow.

"Wait," she swallowed hard, "wait for the next report." As they turned to leave, it was not yet 0400.

They waited for an elevator in silence. When it came, Judith, Brent, and the Rand group got out. Jack and Launa said nothing as they stepped past them. Judith turned in surprise. "Where are you going?"

"To check our gear." Launa's voice came out a harsh whisper.

Judith paled. The elevator door cut off any response.

They changed to shorts and sandals before going to the horses. The bunker was beneath three levels of parking. The trailers sat on the lowest parking level, just above the bunker.

As Launa exited the elevator, she studied the layout. Two ramps led in and out. They had steel doors. Were they airtight?

The wrangler in charge of the horses was not there, so Jack and Launa bridled them. They and the dogs spent the next two hours taking in the cool California morning air.

After their ride, they fed the animals and rubbed down the horses. A quick check in the bunker showed people biting their nails.

Jack took Dr. Harrison aside. "What's the limitations on the transporter?"

"Volume or weight?"

Launa's temper was too short to waste time on minutia. "Which matters?"

Harrison massaged her forehead with a worried hand. "The energy will encapsulate a cylindrical shape. It is tall enough for your horses, but you should hold their heads down. The dogs will fit at your feet. Weight will be your limiter."

"What is the weight limit?" Jack snapped in exasperation.

"We're up to 4,403.16 pounds." Milo jumped in. "If you want to send less, we'll make adjustments."

"I guess we skip lunch," Launa quipped to cool things down.

Jack pulled out a note pad and hurriedly scribbled some numbers. "The dogs, you, me and three horses come to about thirty-six hundred pounds. I've got eight hundred pounds of gear I want to take."

"We take every ounce we can." Launa was with finality.

Harrison nodded. "I'll bring a scale to the lab. We must be precise."

Again, it was hurry up and wait time. They exercised and read Maria's book. The morning went slowly.

At eleven, they collected Brent and Judith for lunch. It was a somber meal. Afterward, Jack stopped by the trailer to have the wrangler take the shoes off the horses.

"I'm not taking iron-shod horses to the bronze age."

"Won't it hurt the horses?" Launa liked walking for exercise, but not as a way of life.

"Hooves are like toenails. They won't feel a thing when the shoes come off. As for shoes, horses only need them to walk on hard-surfaced roads. There won't be many where we're going. Besides, I picked horses with solid, fast-growing hoofs. They'll have less trouble going barefoot than we will."

Launa, Judith and Brent left Jack with the horses while

they went back to the bunker. The communication center was in a world-wide link, but there was nothing, absolutely nothing, coming in.

Jack and Launa spent the afternoon practicing hand-to-hand, quarterstaffs, and knife fighting. The short bronze swords of the Kurgans were no bigger than a Bowie knife. A knife fighter's stance seemed the best way to face them.

Their practice worked up a sweat and kept their minds off things they could do nothing about.

Judith and Brent joined them for supper. They had spent their day selecting an exact target, date, and locale. "We are targeting you to the west of the Danube's mouth," Brent said softly.

Launa had to listen carefully to hear him.

"I just talked to some Romanian friends. They've been digging for the last few summers at what they think was the first village attacked by the Kurgans. Last summer they found a large log in what looked like a carpenter's shop. It had been burned. Between carbon dating the charred edges and studying the rings, we think we've got an exact year for you."

Brent leaned forward over his plate. "If you come across such a log, please leave it in its place. It would be most helpful to us archaeologists."

A faint smile played across Brent's lips. He leaned back in his chair before going on. "We think it was the following spring that the next closest town, about ninety miles further west, was burned. Of course," Brent rubbed his reddened eyes, "any of these dates could be off by as much as five years. I wish I could do better by you."

Judith rested a gentle hand on Brent's elbow. "We are recommending a drop zone eighty miles or so further west from there. We are very sure of that terrain and its contours."

Business complete, conversation faltered. No one was very hungry. The pressure of waiting hung heavy.

After dinner, Judith excused herself. "I'd like to phone my daughter one more time.

Brent stood. "The evening looks nice. I think I'll enjoy a walk and my pipe."

Launa watched her two friends go their separate ways. Was there anyone she needed to hear one last time? Which of her divorced parents should she phone? Either mother or father would fill the call with a litany of perceived wrongs. What comfort would she find in their shallow words as she faced what hung over humanity?

Jack put down his napkin. "I brought a small target from the ranch. How about some archery practice?"

Launa remembered their first sessions with bows and they shared a soft smile.

They kept the range short and spent an hour plunking away. Toward the end, they got goofy. Jack tried trick shots in the negative registry, shooting at 60 or 70 degree angles. "Got to practice getting past shield walls," he quipped.

Launa tried her hand at it and they managed to hit the target a few times. She finished the session feeling loose. The refreshingly cool evening air tip-toed in as the sun sank lower.

Oblivious to humanity's plight, the world showed a vibrant face.

They were pulling the last arrows from the target, when an alarm went off. Moments later, an armed guard ran toward them.

"They're sealing the bunker. You'd better get below," he shouted.

Jack and Launa exchanged glances. There was no need for words. They took one more look at the hills. To the east, another windmill died, slowly winding to a halt. The sky wore the brilliant pastels of the setting sun.

With a long breath, Launa turned and walked back to underground. Mother Earth would receive them, but could she offer them any protection from the twisted toys of her children?

INTERLUDE 4

Bakuza Qwabes raced down the hall, toward the villa's master suite.

Why did he have to be the one to carry this message? Why were there never enough technically trained people among the stalkers? There were plenty of warriors, one of them should carry this message.

Out of breath and trembling with the knowledge he carried, Bakuza burst through the door.

The Leader turned away from a wall hung with spears and war clubs. The previous occupant of the villa had been a collector. A lot of good those ancient weapons would do the Stalkers now.

The Leader fixed Bakuza with blazing eyes.

"You have news of our rocket assault?"

"Yes."

The Leader's eyes narrowed at the missing title, but Bakuza had too little breath for extra words.

"Three of those bastard rockets we modified exploded on the launch pad. The plague is spreading on the wind. All of Africa will have it in days."

"What of Europe?" the Leader snapped, eyes burning.

Bakuza snatched breath in gasps. Hadn't the Leader heard a word about Africa? "Nothing. Not a damn thing. Radio intercepts from the fighters they sent to shoot down our missiles say that our warheads all exploded on entry. We didn't hit a fucking thing."

"They lie." The Leader's eyes were hard as marble.

"European radio and television stations say nothing of our attack. They broadcast like any other day."

"They say only what their government tell them to say."

"My leader, I have lived in America. No one tells reporters what to say." Bakuza's exasperation grew by the second as the Leader refused to face what he had let loose. "You botched it. You set the plague free to ravage Africa and didn't touch the Europeans."

His voice rose to a scream as he tried to get some reaction from the Leader.

He got his reaction.

In the blink of an eye, the Leader plucked a short Zulu thrusting spear from the wall, whirled, and drove it into Qwabes's gut.

Shocked, Bakuza clutched at the spear that impaled him. His gaze traveled along its length, then up to meet the Leader's eyes.

"You can kill the messenger, but you cannot stop the plague."

Bakuza grimaced as the pain seared his gut. "My death will be more pleasant than yours."

The Leader twisted the spear, then yanked it from Qwabes's belly.

Blood gushed over his hands.

Qwabes greeted the darkness gratefully when it came for him.

13

At the elevator, Launa punched the button for the floor their rooms were on. Jack nodded. "I think this calls for a dress uniform. Are we finished with Maria's book on herbs?"

"Hardly."

"Bring it with you."

Fifteen minutes later, showered and in class A's, Jack waited at the elevator. Launa brought the book. With a sanguine smile, Jack took it and punched the UP button.

At the garage, Launa held the elevator while Jack trotted over and stored the book in a sack. Hastening back, he punched for the lowest floor as he said, "We'll find weight for that."

They checked into the bunker and took seats. People huddled in small groups. Launa felt no urge to join them.

She sat quietly, slowly letting her eyes rove the room. Occasionally someone would glance their way, but gradually she and Jack formed an island of quiet in the chaos. A part of her was already detaching herself.

She wondered if dying was like this.

As the screens came to life, Judith came to sit beside Launa. Silently the older woman took Launa's hand and gave it a gentle squeeze. Launa was grateful for the warmth of human touch; a bitter cold was seeping through her veins.

On screen, Launa recognized the American Surgeon General, the first woman to hold the office.

President Lark called the meetings to order. "Admiral Benson, what have you got for us?"

The admiral was in his corner, stooped over fax machines. He picked up a newly arrived message, glanced at it, put it at the bottom of a thick sheaf and walked back to the table.

He stood for a moment, let out a long, tense breath and began. "The agent is fast-acting. People downwind from the launch sites are already sick. Children and elderly have died. Panic is spreading in Africa. Rioting has started."

He put one sheet on the table.

"I don't know how far it will spread. Two hours ago, we recovered the U-2 we sent over Africa. We now have samples of the virus. It's a pretty nasty bug." He bit the edge of his lip as he studied the next fax.

"Our European flights found the virus as low as 30,000 feet. It appears the re-entry vehicles also spread it well above that level."

The admiral turned to the Russian screen. "We appreciate your effort with MiG-31's. Several of them have zoomed to 110,000 feet and returned samples. I regret the loss of one of your aircraft. Did you recover the pilot?"

A Soviet Air Marshall shook his head grimly.

"Those samples have been analyzed. The results are

disquieting," the Admiral coughed softly. "This is outside my expertise. I think the Surgeon General should take over."

The camera zoomed in on the chief American health official. Two faxes rested on the table in front of her. "Mr. President, I was led to expect an AIDS virus." She pointed at the second fax.

"These are not the AIDS virus. What we have here, on the surface, appears to be an influenza virus."

"You mean a flu," the American President interrupted. "We're all sweating a bad cold." He glanced around and laughed. Several others joined him in nervous cackles.

The Surgeon General's cold stare ended the levity before it began.

"Mr. President, I said 'on the surface.' I suspect even the sick genius who constructed these vectors found it impossible to keep AIDS alive in the atmosphere or speed up its slow killing pace. However, they did keep the worst aspect of that virus." She glanced at her notes.

"The normal AIDS virus is a hard case, but a wimp, very weak. A few minutes outside a warm body and it is dead. For years, I have thanked a gracious God for that small favor." The Surgeon General pursed her lips.

"Keep it simple, Doctor." Beside Launa, Judith whispered unheard encouragement to the Surgeon General. "Those airheads won't understand if you go techie on 'em."

"On the outside, it is a simple flu, although one we have not seen since 1983. Because of that, I would not expect anyone to have any immunity left against it. Imbedded in it is a complete set of the RNA for Hepatitis E, a new strain of that disease that does nasty things to the liver, but, like AIDS, is hard to catch and despairingly slow. We have treatment protocols that usually defeat it before it runs its course."

She paused for a moment, lips tight and grim. "Unfortunately, this new virus has a section snipped from the AIDS virus. That portion of RNA orders it to immediately begin replicating rapidly." She paused for a moment to stare at her notes.

No one interrupted her this time.

"You correctly called this a flu virus, Mr. President. As such, it is carried through the air to a victim's lungs. Once on the lungs, it is able to reproduce itself and be coughed back into the air. While the body is quick to resist such deadly viruses as AIDS and requires a massive influx of infection, it takes a more relaxed attitude toward the less deadly diseases such as the common flu. This virus takes advantage of that false appearance to pass through the blood stream to the liver. There, the Hepatitis E enters any cell that is repairing itself. Once there, however, it does not grow slowly as it should, but rapidly, like AIDS. This swiftly destroys the host cell and damages other cells that are then infected." She turned to face the President with sorrowful eyes.

"Somebody has taken two slow killers and created one very fast one," she concluded.

She turned again to ponder her papers. The rooms on the hook up were silent as tombs. Her next words could seal them as such.

"The Soviet flights show much of the virus is succumbing to the solar ultraviolet rays at high altitude. We are coming up on a time of high solar activity. Unfortunately, we are not yet there." She shuffled her papers, glanced at a note. "Indeed, the sun has been quite calm the last few days."

"Damn," came from one of the screens.

"I guess we didn't deplete the ozone layer enough," someone quipped bitterly in Livermore.

"Under normal circumstances, I'd want time for exhaustive tests, but time is something we don't have." She paused to let the full weight of her words sink in.

In Livermore, the room held its collective breath.

"I would expect this virus to be lethal to humans within two to five days of infection, in some cases, less," the Surgeon General said. With those few words, slowly spoken, she pronounced a death warrant for the entire human race.

"No!" The cry burst from so many lips Launa could not tell where it started. On screen, the Surgeon General sat like an iceberg. Nothing betrayed the emotions she felt.

It was several seconds before the president could formulate a question. "Could they be so few bugs that, you know, we won't . . .?"

At that moment, the Surgeon General was handed another fax. She glanced at it, then motioned the admiral over. For half a minute, the two read. When Benson turned away, his head nodded slowly.

"Mr. President, these are the latest reports from the U-2 and MiG-31 flights. I leave it to the doctor to comment on the concentrations they are finding. However, we now have live virus over France, Germany, and the Ukraine as low as 15,000 feet."

The Surgeon General stood up, the only sign of any inner turmoil the nervous rolling of a pen through her fingers. "Mr. President, breathing in a few dozen of these viruses would probably infect your lungs and permit the virus to take hold. In time, enough would pass through your blood to begin the process of destroying all liver function. I see no way to avoid death."

At her words, the meetings disintegrated.

It was several minutes before anyone tried to regain order. Launa sat rigidly in her chair, no longer feeling anything. Judith reached again for her, resting a hand on her lap.

It was the European Prime Minister who shouted the question that caught everyone's attention. "What of the present treatments? Will they have any effect on this new strain?"

The American Surgeon General cleared her throat. "My learned colleagues in Europe may have a different opinion. However, based upon our initial evaluation of this strain, I do not believe any of the existing treatments will prove effective. It replicates too rapidly."

"We regretfully concur." A window opened on a European official. "In time, but of course, we could produce new drugs. But no, not for months, maybe a year or more. How long will we have?" His large round eyes pleaded for time.

The Admiral faced the camera squarely. "The virus is already falling in Europe. The jet stream at higher elevations is moving samples of it eastward at two hundred miles an hour."

"My son's a meteorologist." The Secretary of Commerce interrupted. "He told me the fallout from Chernobyl reached North America in just three or four days." He paused for a moment as the full impact of his words struck home. A stricken look swept his face. "Is that all the time we have?"

"I suggest we remain calm." The Secretary of State leaned forward speaking only inches from his mike. His voice boomed from the speakers. "I understand that we recently had a breakthrough in AIDS treatment. Does that offer a ray of hope?"

The Surgeon General managed a grim smile. "Yes, the serum is effective against any virus, from the common cold to AIDS." Smiles began to appear. There was hope, until she continued softly.

"At this time, we only have enough to treat one patient. It will be several months before we can produce more."

A shudder went through the room.

"So, it seems we can save Adam or Eve, but not both. A sad commentary," the Secretary of State muttered dryly.

Standing beside Launa, Judith muttered. "In 1940, we had enough penicillin to treat President Roosevelt or Prime Minister Churchill for pneumonia, but not both. History repeats itself."

Launa found the phrase 'history repeats itself' repugnant. Like a cold lump of metal in her gut, her resolve grew that this history would not be.

On the three screens, pandemonium broke out.

The Secretary of State again bent next to his microphone, "I suggest we have been inundated with enough information. We would benefit from a break."

Three very deflated Presidents nodded and the screens went blank.

Livermore plunged into darkness as all three screens went black.

"What happened?"

"Did they forget us?" someone cried out.

Before anyone could react, one screen lit up. This one showed the White House Situation Room. Admiral Benson was coming back from the communications center, his face a grim study.

Huddled in his chair, President Lark looked like a puppet whose strings had been slashed.

"How bad is it?" State asked.

"It's spreading faster than I thought. An airliner just landed at Kennedy that probably flew through the cloud when it left Moscow. Aircraft have been crossing Europe and Asia through that damn cloud for the last three hours."

He paused and shook his head. "Folks, we're way behind the power curve on this one."

"Does it matter," the Secretary of Interior offered bitterly, "whether we die in five days or ten?"

The Surgeon General did not say anything. The question had no reply.

Interior turned to the admiral. "You folks in uniform think the unthinkable. What's going to happen?"

The admiral screwed up his face, stared at the ceiling for a moment, then looked at the Surgeon General. "Doctor, no pandemic has ever wiped out more than half of a population. I'm thinking of the medieval plagues."

"Yes," she nodded, "but no one ever engineered so deadly a plague to strike so quickly and so broadly." She presented the facts coldly.

The admiral worried his lower lip. "Does anyone have a natural immunity to Hepatitis E?"

"Even those infected with it are subject to reinfection." She spoke her word so softly it was hard for Launa to taste the absolute finality in it.

Then the monitors faded to gray. "Wait fifteen, Livermore," a disembodied voice instructed them.

No one moved.

Slowly, the reality soaked through Launa. Every hope, every dream, that the human race had fashioned since the beginning of history, would be in ruins before the first heat of summer.

A tear traced its way down her cheek. She felt it slowly fall and held the sensation. That one tear was her donation to the mourning of this future lost.

The rest of her was already changing, hardening into the obsidian that would carve a past regained.

14

The camera lights came back on as the mikes made a popping noise. The monitors showed a subdued cabinet.

"Are you there, Livermore?" The Admiral voice was hard, but empty.

"Yes." Judith reached out to him with a single word.

The Secretary of State turned. "Mr. President?"

The Commander in Chief shook himself. Slowly a glazed stare turned to the Secretary. "Ah, yes. You want, er, something?"

"Yes, Mr. President." State spoke softly. "We've been discussing the time expedition. We recommend you authorize its activation."

"Ah, yeah." The President's eyes wandered unsteadily around the room. "You think things are that bad, Phil?"

"Yes, Mr. President." The Secretary of Defense kept his words gentle, as he might to a child.

"Well, uh, how soon can they do that thing, do you think?" The president's head bobbed up and down, like a boat that had lost its anchor.

The admiral stood up. "Livermore?"

Launa looked to Jack. His breath was coming in strong, deep drafts as he nodded to her to take the honor.

She stood to attention and saluted smartly. "We are ready now, sir."

The admiral returned her salute. After a quick glance in the President's direction, he turned to Launa. "Activate the Neolith Military Advisory Group at your earliest convenience. Be guided by the principle of calculated risk. In matters beyond your briefing, exercise your discretion."

"Yes, sir!" Launa dropped her salute.

Jack joined Launa at attention. Both snapped a salute to the admiral.

"Dismissed, troopers, and Godspeed."

They pivoted smartly and marched from the room.

Jack trailed Launa from the conference room, his gut a knot of contending passions. He was as proud as a warrior and scared as a rabbit. He felt like screaming and running in circles and taking a mountain apart with his bare hands. Was this what his Grandfather had chanted of, the ancient warrior's way?

When Launa came to a halt, he grabbed her by both shoulders. "You did good. Now we make it happen."

She nodded, as solid and cool as steel. "Yes."

Milo and Harrison, Judith and Brent quickly joined them. Emotions fled across their faces as they contended for control of their souls. They stood, staring at one another. There were no words for what passed between them.

Launa broke the silence. "Let's crank 'em up, crew."

The relentless commitment that blazed in her eyes gave

purpose to the civilians. Like the light of a fire, it held their fears at bay, suppressing terror while it burned, giving them purpose, at least for the moment.

Milo turned to Harrison. "Betty, let's warm up the machine. Can't keep these people waiting." They turned to the elevator.

Jack started ticking things off. "We'll need the animals and gear from the trailers."

Harrison turned back. "I had your gear brought down to the transporter when they called the meeting." She halted, embarrassed. "I guess I . . ." She ran out of words.

"Thank you." Launa saved her further discomfort.

"I'll get the horses and dogs," Brent offered.

That was Jack's responsibility. For a second, anger flared, then died as he saw the desperation in Brent's face.

The old man craved action like a drug. Jack surrendered this deed to his friend. Letting him help would help Brent keep at arm's-length the horror that awaited all those left behind.

In silence, they rode up the elevator to the High Energy Unit. Brent continued up alone after they exited. Jack smelled ozone, air conditioning, and hot metal. It tasted bitter.

Their bags were piled on a large scale. He and Launa walked over to it. The digital read-out said exactly 801.52 pounds.

"Damn close." Jack stroked his beard.

"We'll need to weigh ourselves after we change."

He nodded and picked up two small bags that were not on the scales. "This one's yours." He handed it to Launa.

"Does it really matter? One size fits all."

He tried to match her soft banter. "Yeah, but I'd like my own sandals."

To their left the restrooms announced "MEN" and "WOMEN." Obedient to culture, they each went to their door.

Launa stopped, her hand on the door. "I don't want to be by myself," she choked and did not look at Jack.

He turned, wondering if he could force words past the lump closing his throat. "I know. I don't either."

He followed her through the wrong door.

The room was large. Four gray stalls established the boundaries OF civilization. Launa went to the far wall, where three chrome hooks awaited her uniform.

Jack took his coat off, folded it smartly and laid it on the bench at his end of the lavatory. He paused. That green uniform, with its bits of ribbon, cloth, and metal, had been his life for the last ten years.

He would never wear it again.

His throat tightened. A wave of nausea swept over him. He denied it by ripping his tie off, throwing it in a corner. He tore open his shirt, stepped out of his shoes and shed his pants, underwear and socks in a single motion, leaving them in a heap.

Naked, he emptied his bag on the bench and came to a halt with a wry grimace.

It was Launa's bag.

He picked up the sandals, belt, knife, briefs, and turned.

"I seem to have your gear."

Launa had neatly hung her coat and skirt on hooks. Her shoes stood side by side beneath them. She had folded her blouse and bra neatly on the counter and was half out of her pantyhose.

He had to repeat himself.

When she finally turned to him, her eyes were distant.

She said nothing, but pointed to the other bag. Then, folding her hose, she stepped into a stall.

He could hear her emptying her bladder and felt the need himself.

He traded clothing and moved to the furthest stall from her. Both of them might as well have been in armor plate for all the attention they paid each other.

Someday, somewhere, he would pay due homage to the sight of Launa naked and proud as a goddess. Something was wrong with a world where first anger and now emptiness left him with no appetite for such beauty.

L auna sat in the cold privacy of the stall.

In another time, the sight of Jack would have brought feelings. Today, the emptiness inside her swallowed him up unnoticed.

As she worked the cool metal toilet handle, she knew she was touching modern plumbing and probably any modern convenience, for the last time.

Quickly she walked to her gear, belted on the briefs, and tied the sandals.

Jack was waiting, but she took a moment to turn back to her uniform. Softly, she ran her hands down the wool, delighting in its sheen. Her fingers caressed the sharp corners of her gold bars. For most of her life she had dreamed of them.

She had won them and now must give them up. Recklessly, she worked one of the bars from its epaulet and turned to Jack.

He nodded almost imperceptibly as she slipped it into her briefs. She felt as cold as the metal.

Twice, she drew in deep breaths and blew them out. Jack matched her breath for breath. Then, setting her face, she squared her shoulders.

Jack opened the door. Wrapping herself in decision, she strode forward purposefully, whether as convicted to execution or hero to adventure, the next moments would tell.

Harrison stood beside the empty scales. The horses were laden. Launa and Jack paced off the distance to the scales together.

The doctor read the numbers and fed her hand-held calculator. "You're eighty-three point four pounds short of forty-four hundred and three pounds."

Jack pointed to a satchel near the horse wrangler. "Make up the balance from there."

A technician brought it, draw out gold nuggets and leaf, and placed them on the scales. It did not surprise Launa; she was beyond feelings. A few moments later, she and Jack held two soft leather pouches with the measured weight in gold.

They moved to the animals.

Star nuzzled Launa. Windrider and Big Red greeted Jack with soft nickers. Frieda, Mist and Alert softly rubbed against their legs. This was the least rambunctious greeting Launa could remember from the dogs.

"I slipped some tranquilizers into the horses' and dogs' feed," the wrangler offered by way of explanation. "It'll wear off in an hour, but it should help them now."

He handed Launa two of the dog leashes, Jack the other.

Launa wanted no long good-byes. The numbness that allowed her to keep going might pass at any moment. She respected the tight control the Livermore crew kept over whatever demons hounded them.

Launa turned to Milo. She thought to salute him and say

something historic, but the vision of herself, naked and vulnerable, trying to act like a Prussian automaton, made for poor theater. She set her jaw resolutely.

"Let's get this show on the road, shall we, doc?" She sounded like her old man did after packing the car for a weekend trip. For a moment, she feared she had blown it, but the tight grin on Jack's face gave assurance.

As Milo bent to his instruments, Judith came to stand between them. "If something happens and the situation stabilizes at an acceptable level, we'll attempt to bring you back."

Launa swallowed hard. "We'll stand by the drop zone for a week, doing as little as possible. If you can't recover us, send a message canceling the mission. We'll slaughter the animals, destroy, burn, or bury the gear, and do the same with ourselves. We won't allow our lives to risk damage to history if things go okay here."

Launa's gut knotted at her first life and death order.

Grimly, Jack nodded assent.

Milo looked up. "We're ready. A short countdown, from five, on my mark. Okay?"

He looked around; no one objected. Launa took a deep breath and began tightening her muscles, legs, then stomach, then arms, preparing for whatever might come.

"Mark." Doctor Milo started counting. "Five. Four. Three."

The dogs twitched nervously, whined. The horses tossed their heads, shuffled their hoofs, fought their bridles. Launa pulled tight on the animals' leads. Remembering her parachute training, she relaxed her legs.

"Two. One. Go."

The count ended.

Launa gave a final look to the laboratory, the beige walls, the white smocked technicians, the gleaming metal and gray equipment.

Then things began to get hazy.

ABOUT THE AUTHOR

Mike Shepherd also writes the national bestselling Kris Longknife saga.

He grew up Navy. It taught him early about change and the chain of command. He's worked as a bartender and cab driver, personnel advisor and labor negotiator. Now retired from building databases about the endangered critters of the Pacific Northwest, he's looking forward to some fun reading and writing.

Mike lives in Vancouver, Washington, with his wife Ellen, and is close to his daughter and grandchildren. He enjoys reading, writing, dreaming, watching grandchildren for story ideas, and upgrading his computer; all are never-ending.

For more information:
www.mikeshepherd.org
mikeshepherd@krislongknife.org

2017 RELEASES

In 2016, I amicably ended my twenty-year publishing relationship with Ace, part of Penguin Random House.

In 2017, I began publishing through my own independent press, KL & MM Books.

I am delighted to say that you fans have responded wonderfully. We have sold over 20,000 copies of the five e-novels. In 2018, I intend to keep the novels coming,

We started the year with **Kris Longknife's Replacement** that tells the story of Grand Admiral Sandy Santiago as she does her best as a mere mortal to fill the shoes left behind on Alwa Station by Kris Longknife. Sandy has problems galore: birds, cats, and vicious alien raiders. Oh, and she's got Rita Nuu-Longknife as well!

February had a novelette. **Kris Longknife: Among the Kicking Birds** was part of Kris Longknife: Unrelenting. However, it went long and these four chapters were cut to one short paragraph. I hope you enjoy the full story.

Rita Longknife: Enemy Unknown was available in March and is the first book of the long-awaited Iteeche War series. Rita has had enough of Ray Longknife gallivanting around the universe. No sooner is little Al born, than ships start disappearing. Is it pirates or something more sinister? Rita gets herself command of a heavy cruiser, some nannies, and heads out to see what there is to see.

April had another short offering, **Kris Longknife's Bad Day**. You just knew when Kris asked for a desk job that she'd have days like you have at the office. Well, here's one that will bring you up to date on the technical developments in the Royal US Navy, as well as silly bureaucratic goings on. In the first draft of **Emissary**, these were the opening chapters, but I found a better opening and this got cut. Enjoy!

Kris Longknife: Emissary began an entirely new story arc for Kris and was available May 1. Here is the story of what it takes to get Kris out from behind a desk. And for those of you betting in the pool, you'll get your answer. More I cannot say.

June brought you Abby Nightingale's view of things around Alwa in **Kris Longknife's Maid Goes on Strike.** You knew sooner or later this was going to happen.

July had another book set in Alwa. As **Kris Longknife's Relief,** Sandy Santiago, continues to battle aliens of various persuasions and not a few humans.

Rita Longknife: Enemy in Sight was released in September and sought to resolve the unknowns left by Enemy Unknown as humanity slipped backwards into a war it does not want and may not be able to win.

Kris Longknife's Maid Goes on Strike and Other Short Stories, is a collection of four short stories: Maid Goes on Strike, Ruthie Longknife's First Christmas, Among the Kicking Birds, and Bad Day. These were available in October all under one ebook cover for a great price.

Kris Longknife: Admiral was available in November. In this adventure, Kris is up to her ears in warships, enemies, and friendlies who may be not as friendly as she'd like, as battlecruisers square off against battlecruisers. A fight where both sides are equal is a bloody fight that often no one wins.

Work is already going on for a January 18 release of Kris Longknife's Successor. March will have the next book in the Iteeche War, and May will continue Kris's adventures in the Iteeche Empire with Kris Longknife: Warrior.

Stay in touch to follow developments by following Kris Longknife on Facebook or checking in at my website www.mikeshepherd.org.

I hope to soon have a mailing list you can sign up for.

2018 RELEASES

In 2016, I amicably ended my twenty-year publishing relationship with Ace, part of Penguin Random House.

In 2017, I began publishing through my own independent press, KL & MM Books. We produced six e-books and a short story collection. We also brought the books out in paperback and audio.

In 2018, I intend to keep the novels coming.

We will begin the year with **Kris Longknife's Successor**. Grand Admiral Santiago still has problems. Granny Rita is on the rampage again, and the cats have gone on strike, refusing to send workers to support the human effort on Alwa. Solving that problem will be tough. The last thing Sandy needs is trouble with the murderess alien space raiders. So, of course, that is what she gets.

May 1 will see **Kris Longknife: Commanding**. Kris has won her first battle, but the way the Iteeche celebrate victory can be hard on the stomach. The rebellion won't quit and now Kris needs to raise a fleet, not only to defend the Iteeche Imperial Capitol, but also take the war to the rebels.

In the second half of 2018, you can look forward to the next Vicky Peterwald novel on July 1, another Iteeche war novel on September 1, and **Kris Longknife Implacable** on November 1.

Stay in touch to follow developments by friending Kris Longknife and follow Mike Shepherd on Facebook or check in at my website www.krislongknife.com

Made in the USA
Middletown, DE
22 August 2019